stake that!

*Berkley JAM Titles by Mari Mancusi*

STAKE THAT!

BOYS THAT BITE

# stake that!

## Mari Mancusi

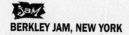
BERKLEY JAM, NEW YORK

THE BERKLEY PUBLISHING GROUP
Published by the Penguin Group
Penguin Group (USA) Inc.
375 Hudson Street, New York, New York 10014, USA
Penguin Group (Canada), 90 Eglinton Avenue East, Suite 700, Toronto, Ontario M4P 2Y3, Canada
(a division of Pearson Penguin Canada Inc.)
Penguin Books Ltd., 80 Strand, London WC2R 0RL, England
Penguin Group Ireland, 25 St. Stephen's Green, Dublin 2, Ireland (a division of Penguin Books Ltd.)
Penguin Group (Australia), 250 Camberwell Road, Camberwell, Victoria 3124, Australia
(a division of Pearson Australia Group Pty. Ltd.)
Penguin Books India Pvt. Ltd., 11 Community Centre, Panchsheel Park, New Delhi—110 017, India
Penguin Group (NZ), Cnr. Airborne and Rosedale Roads, Albany, Auckland 1310, New Zealand
(a division of Pearson New Zealand Ltd.)
Penguin Books (South Africa) (Pty.) Ltd., 24 Sturdee Avenue, Rosebank, Johannesburg 2196,
South Africa

Penguin Books Ltd., Registered Offices: 80 Strand, London WC2R 0RL, England

STAKE THAT!

This book is an original publication of The Berkley Publishing Group.

This is a work of fiction. Names, characters, places, and incidents either are the product of the author's imagination or are used fictitiously, and any resemblance to actual persons, living or dead, business establishments, events, or locales is entirely coincidental. The publisher does not have any control over and does not assume any responsibility for author or third-party websites or their content.

PRINTING HISTORY
Berkley JAM trade paperback edition / December 2006

Library of Congress Cataloging-in-Publication Data

Mancusi, Marianne.
    Stake that! / Mari Mancusi.—Berkley Jam trade paperback ed.
       p. cm.
    Summary: Still reeling from having lost her chance to become a vampire, sixteen-year-old Rayne learns that she is destined to be the new vampire slayer and must go undercover to stop a maniacal member of the undead who seeks vengeance and power by spreading a fatal blood disease.
    ISBN 0-425-21210-6
    [1. Vampires—Fiction. 2. Virus diseases—Fiction. 3. Goth culture (Subculture)—Fiction. 4. Twins—Fiction. 5. Sisters—Fiction. 6. Single-parent families—Fiction.] I. Title.
    PZ7.M312178Sta 2006
    [Fic]—dc22

                                                                                         2006025846

PRINTED IN THE UNITED STATES OF AMERICA

10  9  8  7  6  5  4  3  2  1

*To the "Summer Bites Street Team"*
*and all my MySpace friends.*
*You guys rock!!!*

# 1

## BLOGFAST SUX!!!!!!!!!

OMG I am sooo pissed right now!

As you know, I've been keeping this blog for like EVER in an effort to document my transformation into a vampire. I've shared with you my notes from my Vamp Certification 101 class, told you all the juicy details about my hot vampire blood mate-to-be, Magnus. Heck, I've even posted excerpts from the *Biting Humans for Fun and Profit* manual.

But what does my blogging site decide to do the week everything is supposed to go down? IT decides to go down, TOO! The whole last week's worth of entries . . . vanished into thin cyberspace air. *Grrrrrrrrr!!!!!*

*Okay, deep breath, Rayne. There's nothing you can do*

*about it except send threatening hate e-mail to Blogfast.com. And then the vindictive little geeks who run the site will probably delete your whole blog altogether instead of just last week's entries. Better to just recap and deal.*

But still. Major *grrr*, if you ask me.

Okay. Of course you're all dying to know: Am I a vampire? After all, the last blog entry of my own *Neverending Story* not eaten by The Nothing was written the night I was scheduled to be transformed. I was headed to Club Fang (the coolest Goth club in the known universe) with my twin sister, Sunny. (Yes, yes, we're Sunshine and Rayne. Hippie parents and all that. And we've already heard all the jokes, so please don't bother.) There I was to meet my blood mate, the drool-worthy vampire Magnus. He was supposed to bite me and then we'd spend eternal life together as vampires, which, FYI, is a pretty sweet gig. I mean, we're talking riches beyond belief, amazing powers, and best of all NO HIGH SCHOOL. w00t!

Problem is that's not exactly how it all went down. Instead of biting me, Magnus the Mentally Challenged bit my twin sister, Sunny, instead. We're like, identical, you know, but still! You'd think he would at least have double-checked that he had the right girl before going to the point of no return. After all, we're talking Real Life Extinguishing Event here, not some *Parent Trap* movie starring Lindsay Puke Lohan.

And let me tell you, Sunny, who had no idea up until then that the whole vamp world even existed, was *so* not pleased to be informed that due to a "bloody" bad case of mistaken identity she would now spend eternity as a pasty, blood-gulping creature of the night. (Her words, not mine!) And Magnus the Moron was freaked out beyond belief that he was going to get in trouble with the boss, Lucifent, for performing an unauthorized bite. (After all, she wasn't even blood tested first for diseases. Not that my innocent little twin sis would ever have diseases!) Luckily for Maggy, Lucifent got dusted soon after by Bertha the Vampire Slayer. So Mag not only got off scot-free, he became the new Master of the Blood Coven and high priest of the eastern vampire conglomerate of the United States of America. Life is strange.

So, long story (somewhat) short, the two of them decided to see if they could stop the transformation. Ended up having to go to England to get a drop of pure blood from the Holy Grail. It's too long and boring to tell, but I made Sunny promise to write it all down so maybe when she does I can post it here or something. Bottom line: They were able to stop the vamp process and my sweet little sis is now a member of the human race again. Of course, in the process, her and Magnus fell deeply in love and now they're doing the interspecies dating thing.

Which leaves me back at square one. No hot blood mate to spend eternity with. No riches beyond belief. Just an American

History paper that I didn't write because I'd assumed I'd be an immortal dropout before the due date. Can we say, "Rayne's Life Sucks Big Time?"

Bleh. I'm too depressed to write. More later.

**POSTED BY RAYNE McDONALD @ 8:30 A.M.**
**THREE COMMENTS:**

**Ashleigh says . . .**
OMG, Rayne! That totally sux that Blogfast ate ur entries. U should, like, totally sue or something. I was on vacation with the fam & figured I'd catch up on ur adventures when I came back and now I've missed everything! Booooooo!!

**ButterfliQT says . . .**
Thank god your sis got 2 turn back 2 a human! From what you've written about her, I think she'd make a totally sucky vamp!!!! (LOL—sucky vamp! hehe)

**Rayne says . . .**
I'm sooo with you, Butterfli. I mean, the girl didn't appreciate the idea of immortal life and big bucks one bit! She was more interested in who was gonna take her to the prom. Puh-leeze.

**DarkGothBoy says . . .**

Hey. U R Hot. Screw Magnus. He sounds like a tool. I'll be your blood mate any day. IM me—DarkGothBoy.

**Rayne says . . .**

WhatEVER, dude. I'm looking for a REAL vampire, not some poseur who gets off on blood suckage.

# 2

## Drama with the Drama Teacher

You are *never* going to believe what happened to me today. So it's Monday. And I'm walking through the hallways of Oakridge High, feeling pretty good about myself, right? I mean, I decided to try to have a positive attitude about the whole thing. Sure, I missed my op to become a vamp this time around and had to get back on the waiting list for the next blood mate, but it wasn't like I'd lost my chance forever. And besides, Magnus may be hot, but he's so not the type of guy I'd want to spend eternity with. (I want someone *waaaaaay* more dark and brooding.) So in a way, I figured, it all worked out for the best.

So, as I was saying . . . I'm walking through the halls, giving the finger to various meathead jocks like Mike Stevens—football quarterback and loser extraordinaire—avoiding the teachers who want to put me in detention for skipping class to go smoke over at "The Block," flirting with the new kid wearing an Interpol shirt. (He's not that cute, but evidently has good taste in music.) You know, your typical Raynie day.

Then suddenly, out of nowhere, some random old guy grabs me on the arm and starts dragging me into a side corridor.

"You must come with me," he says in an urgent voice.

I'm just about ready to go tae kwon do on his ass, but then I realize it's Mr. Teifert, Sunny's drama coach.

"Dude, I think you've gotten me mistaken for my twin," I say, as he drags me down into the auditorium's backstage area. "I'm Rayne. Sunny's the one in your play, not me." This mistaken-for-my-twin thing has so gotta stop.

The teacher pulls on the door and it slams closed with a large ominous clanking sound. Which, FYI, is a totally cool sound effect. I could use that in my next film. (For those of you just joining us, I'm going to be the next Tim Burton or David Lynch, just FYI.)

"I know who you are, Rayne," Mr. Teifert says, scratching his balding head.

I raise an eyebrow. "Oh. Then maybe an explanation of why you hauled me in here might be in order, do you think?"

He nods. "Yes, yes, of course." He takes a deep breath. "Now brace yourself. This may be a little difficult to take in . . ."

At first I totally think he's going to come up with some sicko declaration of love or something. Which would have been extremely gross. I mean, sure, I dated my English teacher for two weeks last semester, but he was a twenty-two-year-old sexy Australian who liked Nietzsche. Mr. Teifert's practically ancient—at least forty, I'd say—and so not sexy or cute or Australian. Besides, once I caught him singing show tunes, so I've been thinking he might bat for the other team.

"What I'm going to tell you may come as a bit of a shock," he continues in an extremely serious tone.

Jeez, enough with the drama, drama teacher guy.

"Shock. Awe. I gotcha. Spit it out." After all, I'm late for class. Not that this would normally bother me.

He clears his throat. "Very well then. Once a generation there is a girl born who is destined to slay the vampires."

I stare at him. "You know about Bertha the Vampire Slayer?" I ask incredulously. "You know about vampires?" Okay, he's right. I am shocked. And awed. And all that. I had no idea this nerdy old teacher had any clue about the Otherworld. I guess that's why he acted so weird when Sunny and I were joking around in the auditorium last week.

"Bertha, um, has had some blood pressure issues," he stammers. "She's temporarily retired from the slaying biz."

"I see . . ." I say slowly. Too much drive-thru SuperSizing for Bertha between slays, I guess.

"No, I don't think you do," Mr. Teifert says. "What I'm trying to tell you, Ms. McDonald, is that you are next in line."

"Next in line?" I swallow hard, not liking where this is going. "Next in line for what, exactly?" I mean, sure, if he's going to say next in line for the senior class play iPod give-away, I'm his girl. But somehow I think he might be going in a much more unpleasant and less tuneful direction.

Mr. Teifert's smile doesn't quite reach his eyes as he holds out his hand. I stare down at it, not ready to shake.

"Congratulations Rayne McDonald," he says. "You are the chosen one. Slayer Inc.'s new official vampire slayer."

I gape. "What the—"

Oh, crap. My mom's calling me to dinner. More later . . .

**POSTED BY RAYNE McDONALD @ 5 P.M.**
**THREE COMMENTS:**

**Angelbaby3234566 says** . . .
OMG, Rayne! How can u leave us hanging?!?! Come back and tell us the rest! How can u be a vampire slayer?????

**DarkGothBoy says . . .**

Hey—serves you right, you snotty beeyotch. Now you'll WISH you hooked up with me. No vamp will touch you with a ten-foot pole. Sux2BU.

**Rayne says . . .**

Don't worry, GothBoy—I'd rather become a nun than touch your, um, pole.

# 3

## Destiny Bites!

'm back. Sorry for the interruption. Mom has been militant about the whole family eating together ever since Dad left us. (Don't even get me started!) She would have freaked if I didn't show up for our nightly meal of tofu burgers and baked cardboard—er, French fries. I think she gets lonely, especially now that Sunny and I have a car and we're always off doing our own thing. She needs to start dating again. I mean, she's a total hippie—but seems downright Quaker when it comes to free love.

Anyway, back to "the slayer" thing.

I stare at Mr. Teifert. "Sorry dude," I say. "I so cannot become the slayer. No freaking way. I mean, I'm in the vamp inner circle here. I have vampire friends. My sister is dating the new Blood Coven Master vamp. I'm on the waiting list to become a vampire myself. How can you expect me to all of a sudden go all Terminator on them? That just doesn't fit into the Rayne five-year plan."

There are several armchairs on stage, set up for the production of the senior class play *Bye Bye Birdie* (which Sunny is starring in, BTW). Mr. Teifert motions for me to sit in one of them, but I shake my head. I'm not interested in sitting around and chatting with this psycho.

"I'm so out of here," I say, turning to exit stage left.

"Wait," he calls after me. "You must listen to what I have to say."

"Dude, I don't have to listen to a damn thing," I retort, but something inside me makes me stop walking. Curiosity, I guess. I mean, desirable occupation or no, it's not every day one gets told one has a "destiny." Especially by the drama coach.

Mr. Teifert sighs, running a hand through his wild black hair. "Actually, you do, Rayne."

"What's that supposed to mean?"

"I'll tell you, if you'll sit."

*Grr.* I mean, what am I, a dog or something? I reluctantly turn back and head toward center stage. I plop down in the nearest chair, which is way more uncomfortable than it looks. The springs dig into my butt and I hope this big revelation of my destiny isn't going to take too long.

"So tell me already," I say.

Mr. Teifert takes the seat across from me. He leans forward, hands on his knees. "You know me as a high school teacher. But I am also senior vice president of Slayer Inc. We're a human-run organization that tracks the vampire community and makes sure they stay in line."

"And if they don't, you dust them. Very diplomatic."

Mr. Teifert sighs. "Yes. There are times when that becomes our only option. But we do try to use other, more civilized methods first."

"Um-hm."

"But if all else fails, if the vampire in question refuses to follow the code, then we must remove him."

"Like you did with Lucifent?" I accuse, remembering how Bertha the Vampire Slayer recently took down the former master. "What did he ever do to you?"

Teifert shifts, as if his seat is suddenly uncomfortable. "That's confidential," he says. "But trust me, we had our reasons."

"Okay, fine," I say. Obviously this was going nowhere. "Not that I agree with your methods, but let's move on. So if, like, once a generation there's a slayer born and Bertha is that slayer in mine, how come you're picking on me?"

Teifert snorts. "Please. This is the twenty-first century. You don't think we'd have a backup?" He shakes his head. "Sure, in the old days they only chose one. But then when that one was killed by a vampire or something they had to wait a whole other generation before they could start policing the covens again. Completely impractical. So nowadays we select several girls at birth."

"So if I die in my duties, you just swap me out? Kind of harsh." Suddenly I have sympathy for Bertha.

"Our goal is, of course, to keep you alive. And we will do everything in our power to do that."

"You're talking like I've already agreed to do this," I point out. "I haven't. And I won't, actually. I'm on a waiting list to become a vampire and I'm thinking that becoming an official slayer would definitely put me at the back of the line."

"I'm sorry, Rayne," Mr. Teifert says, in actuality not sounding the least bit apologetic. "But you don't have a choice."

I narrow my eyes. "What do you mean 'I don't have a choice'? *Of course* I have a choice. I can just, like, choose. To slay vampires or to let them live. And I choose life. Well, not life exactly, seeing as they're technically already dead. Undead, I guess, but—"

"When you were born, you were injected with a dormant nanovirus by a Slayer Inc. operative working in Mercy Hospital," Mr. Teifert interrupts in an oddly calm voice. "If you refuse to fulfill your destiny, we will be forced to activate the virus and you will, I'm afraid, suffer a very painful death."

I'm sure my eyes are totally bugging out of my head now as I stare at him. Nanovirus? WTF is a nanovirus? He's gotta be kidding, right? I glance around the auditorium, looking for Ashton Kutchner telling me I'm being Punk'd. This has got to be a joke, right?

I realize my palms are totally sweaty all of a sudden. And my fingers have become real trembly. Fear pokes at my heart. Has Teifert already activated the virus? Am I dying as we speak? OMG, I could be literally dying. Right here, right now!

Or am I just being all Hypochondriac Girl? Like the time I swore I had come down with Ebola after reading about it in Social Studies. I mean, I had all the symptoms. Headache, muscle ache, red eyes, fatigue, stomach pain . . .

The school nurse had not been impressed, informing me that those were also symptoms of a hangover. As was the distinct smell of vodka on my breath. Guess I should have brushed my teeth a few more times after Spider and I embarked on our "do these fake IDs work" adventure the night before.

But I'm not taking any chances. Especially since it feels like my throat is starting to close up. My vision is getting spotty. "Please!" I beg. "I want to live. Turn it off! Please, turn it off!"

Mr. Teifert rolls his eyes. "I haven't turned it on, Rayne. But I must say I am quite impressed by your dramatic prowess. Ever consider the theater?"

Oh.

Vision returns. Throat loosens. I no longer feel the urge to go toward the light. Phew.

"Come with me." Mr. Teifert rises from his chair and beckons me to follow. I reluctantly stand up and trail behind him as he heads to the back of the stage, behind the cheerily painted background flats, behind the interior curtain, behind the cage that holds all the lighting controls. Just when I think we can't go back any farther, we come to a small, nondescript door I'd never noticed before.

Mr. Teifert pulls out a large old-fashioned golden key and slips it into the lock. Before opening the door, he glances from left to right. To see if we're alone, I guess. Then he turns the key. The door creaks open.

I can practically feel my heart pounding against my chest cavity as I follow him inside. At this point I'm thinking, what if the guy just made up the whole Slayer Inc. thing? What if he's really some psycho axe-wielding teacher who likes to chop up teenagers and then eat them in the back room? Have any other students gone missing from Oakridge lately? Hm. When was the last time I saw Tubby Toby? He had a lot of meat on his bones . . .

I'm about ready to run screaming back onto the stage, when Teifert flips a switch and the room becomes bathed in a dull orange glow. I glance around, my breath catching in my throat. Suddenly, I'm too fascinated to leave, even if I now have an even better reason to do so.

Weapons. Lots of weapons. In fact, I'd bet my Dr. Marten combat boot collection that none of you have seen so many weapons in one place before. (Well, if you don't count museums, which I don't, as those are ancient weapons behind glass. Not the ready-to-chop-off-someone's-head-at-a-moment's-notice variety like these are.) There are intricate medieval swords, shiny axes (gulp!), and a large collection of jeweled daggers.

"Tools of the slayer," Teifert explains. I glance over at him. Under this lighting he no longer looks like a dorky drama teacher. In fact, if I didn't know better, I'd say he had some kind of weird glow about him. A glow of . . . power.

"I can use these?" I ask, running a hand along the helm of the sword. I start imagining myself wielding the mighty blade. Just like that cool senior Jen Taufman who belongs to the Society of Creative Anachronism and does medieval battle recreations on the weekends.

"Uh, no," Mr. Teifert corrects, sinking all my dreams of becoming a twenty-first-century knight in shining armor. Figures. He pulls open a drawer and rummages around. "Not right away, anyway. To begin with, you'll use this."

I stare at the item in his hand. That? That's all I get to vanquish evil and slay immortal creatures of the night?

"Uh, that's just a chunk of wood, dude."

"It's a stake," Mr. Teifert clarifies. "You must know about staking vampires, Rayne. Even Hollywood's got that part right."

I roll my eyes. "But those stakes are at least smooth. Pointy. Elegant almost. I bet you just found that thing outside on the ground in the woods."

Mr. Teifert inspects the rough stick in his hand. "That's because it's not finished yet. Each slayer must carve her own stake. Embed it with her own essence. That's what gives it its power."

"Oh, joy. So not only do I have to go out and fight evil villains, but I have to take up woodworking, too?"

The drama teacher sighs deeply. "I never said becoming the slayer would be a field trip to a Backstreet Boys concert."

"Good. Because I'd rather stab myself with an unfinished stake than attend one of those," I inform him. "Die a slow painful death. It'd still be better. I can't believe you think I'd like a band like that. I mean, I know you adults all think we teens look the same, but hello?" I gesture to my outfit. "Black-wearing, night-worshipping Goth girl here. I so have better taste than that."

"Um, right. We're getting off topic here," Teifert interrupts. Good thing, too, cause I had a lot more to say on the subject. I mean, talk about insulting!

The drama coach holds out the stake. I take it, reluctantly, worried that the nasty thing is going to give me splinters.

"Um, thanks," I mutter, not quite sure of the appropriate response to the giftage of a piece of wood.

"Look, Rayne. Try to see the job as an opportunity," Teifert tries again. Jeez. The man doesn't give up. He'd make a great Army recruiter.

"An opportunity to murder innocent creatures of the night that pose absolutely no threat to the human race? Rock on." There's more than a hint of sarcasm in my voice, as you can probably imagine.

"Now that's where you're mistaken, little girl," Mr. Teifert says, narrowing his eyes and going all authority figure on me. "Not all vampires are so-called 'good guys,' as you seem to believe. And those who are live a peaceful existence have no reason to fear our organization. It's only the evil vampires that we wish to keep in line."

"Okay, fine. Only the bad guys. What about my sister's boyfriend?" I ask. "Is Magnus a goodie or a baddie?"

"We are pleased at Magnus's rise to power. We feel he will be a great master, actually."

Oh. Well that's a relief. Don't have to worry about pissing Sunny off. Nanovirus or not, dusting one's sister's BF would so be against the twin code of honor.

"Okay. So if I were to take this gig," I say cautiously. "Not that I'm necessarily saying yes, but if I do, who'd be my first victim?"

Mr. Teifert reaches into his leather briefcase and pulls out a file. He flips through the pages until he comes to an eight-by-ten photo. He holds it up so I can take a look.

My eyes widen and a chill trips down my spine as I examine the photo. The vamp in question just looks evil. Seriously evil. He has jet-black hair—parted down the middle and hanging to his shoulders—a trim goatee, pure white skin, and piercing ice-blue eyes that seem to bore into my skull. Sort of resembles Trent Reznor from Nine Inch Nails. If Trent had huge fangs protruding from his bloodred lips, that is.

"Maverick," Mr. Teifert whispers.

The name has power. Like the bad guy in *Harry Potter*. Hearing it sends chills down my spine. I stare at the picture. The eyes seem to taunt me. Begging me to come closer . . . closer . . .

"Okay, okay!" I cry, turning my head away. "I've seen enough."

Mr. Teifert slips the picture back into the file. "Maverick owns the Blood Bar downtown. It's an underground nightclub where humans can go and pay to have their blood sucked by a vampire."

"Um?" I raise an eyebrow. "Ew?" I mean, I'm a big fan of all things vamp, but that just sounds creepy and wrong.

"Yes. 'Ew' would be an appropriate reaction, I think. It's not exactly a high-class establishment. Strictly for the extreme fetish crowd."

"So people get off on that? Getting sucked dry by a vamp turns them on?"

"Evidently. It's become quite the hot spot."

"And you want to shut them down."

"Not exactly. While we don't approve, as a rule, of these un-licensed bite shops, we understand that humans are doing this of their own free will, making it a victimless crime. And nor-mally the vamps that work there are all tested for diseases be-fore becoming employed. So while it's a bit . . . distasteful . . . we tend to turn a blind eye."

"Then what . . . ?"

"Maverick has been very vocal about his displeasure at Magnus taking over the Blood Coven after Lucifent's death. We believe he may be up to something. We need you to infil-trate the Blood Bar. Pose as a human who'd like to get sucked. Figure out what Maverick has planned and then, if you get the opportunity, stake him."

Huh. That doesn't sound so bad actually. In a way, I'd be helping the vamps. The good guys anyway. And saving the life of my twin's BF. I'd be a hero. Maybe my good deeds would actually push me to the front of the vampire line. Then Slayer Inc. could just get the next chick in line to be the once-a-generation slayer.

Also, there's that whole nanovirus in my bloodstream thing that's awfully convincing. Well, if that's even true. Which it might not be. Come to think of it, it does seem a tad far-fetched, don't you think? Like some story an adult would make up to get a teen to do whatever he says. Still, I'm not taking any chances 'til I find out for sure. Maybe Magnus will know the deal.

I square my shoulders, firming my resolve. "Okay," I say, hoping I sound more brave than I feel. "I'll do it."

**POSTED BY RAYNE McDONALD @ 7 P.M.**
**FOUR COMMENTS:**

**CandyGrrl says . . .**
OMG, Rayne! That's so crazy! I can't believe u of all people r now the slayer! Ur like some superhero or something! Do u get powers like Buffy? And more important, do u get to hook up with Spike? Yum!

**Rayne says . . .**
Hm . . . dunno about the powers. Forgot to ask. As for Spike, I certainly wouldn't kick him out of bed if he were to crawl in one night. ☺

**TheyROut2GetMe says . . .**
Don't you think it's a little dangerous to post your "secret" mission on your blog for everyone in the known universe to read? I mean, what if Maverick Googles himself and learns about your plans?

**Rayne says . . .**

Uh, hello?! You think I'm stupid? You don't think I changed names to protect the innocent—or the guilty in this case? [Though Maverick is a way-cool name for an evil vampire, don't you think? I named him after this author I dig.] And the Blood Bar's real name is much more creative and Gothy sounding. But yeah, "Maverick" can Google himself until the bats come home—he ain't stumbling across my blog.

# 4

## Gamer Grrls

t's wicked late—just popped on for a minute. Was playing World of Warcraft—this online video game—with Spider, my best friend. Spider plays a gnome mage (like a pint-size magician) and I play this fierce human warrior chick. It's the best game EVER and we play all the time. Mom claims I'm totally addicted, but, hey, I could say the same to her about her repeated watchings of BBC's *Pride and Prejudice*. She <3's Colin Firth with a vengeance.

Anyway I told Spider about the whole slayer thing over chat. Rather then recapping, I'll just paste in the transcript:

**RAYNIEDAY:** OMG, Spider, the weirdest thing happened today!

**SPIDER:** The cheerleaders invited you to join their ranks?

**RAYNIEDAY:** Um, no.

**SPIDER:** Football captain Mike Stevens asked you out?

**RAYNIEDAY:** Heh. No. And uh, ew, BTW.

**SPIDER:** Then I'm sorry, it's not the weirdest thing. Maybe it's up there in weirdness, sure, I'll buy that. But THE weirdest thing? I think not.

**RAYNIEDAY:** Hehe. This is even weirder. I'm telling you.

**SPIDER:** Watch out behind you! An orc!

*\*\*Spider casts fireball on Orc. 450 damage.*
*\*\*Rayne slashes at Orc. Orc dodges her blow.*
*\*\*Orc hits Spider for 1,324 damage.*
*\*\*Spider dies.*

**SPIDER:** D'oh! I hate being the mage. I'm always the first to die. How come you never die? I'm the one doing ALL the damage and you just rack up the experience points.

**RAYNIEDAY:** 'Cause I'm wearing armor. Duh. You're going into battle wearing, like, some silk robe. Hello?

**SPIDER:** Yeah, I'm, like, freaking tissue paper here. Come get the mage, everyone. Pick on the poor squishy mage!

**RAYNIEDAY:** ANYWAY—while you run back from the grave-yard, I've got to tell you what happened!!!
**SPIDER:** Hmph. No sympathy. Fine. Fine.

So I tell Spider about Mr. Teifert. Slayer Inc. My destiny. Etc., etc.

**SPIDER:** Wow. That's so crazy. What are you going to do?
**RAYNIEDAY:** IDK. Slay Maverick, I guess? I mean, if he's out to get Sunny's BF, then that seems like the right thing to do.
**SPIDER:** But isn't that totally dangerous? I mean, what if you get made into a bloody snack?
**RAYNIEDAY:** Gulp. Thanks. You're making me feel so much better.
**SPIDER:** Just trying to be realistic.
**RAYNIEDAY:** I know, but I, like, don't have a choice here. They've got the nanos in me. If I don't help them, they'll kill me. And I'd so rather be a living snack than dead meat.
**SPIDER:** Guess you've got a point there. Still, be careful, okay? I mean infiltrating a vamp nest and trying to stake their evil leader? That sounds harder than passing Trig without sleeping with the teacher.
**RAYNIEDAY:** Heh. So THAT'S your secret. :P
**SPIDER:** Hehe. I don't "sine" and tell.

**RAYNIEDAY:** Very "cosine."

**SPIDER:** At least I don't go off on "tangents."

**RAYNIEDAY:** Uh-huh. ANYWAY—I'm going to head to the Blood Bar 2morrow nite. I'll IM you when I get back, k? If I don't IM, tell Sunny what happened and maybe Magnus can send in the big guns.

**SPIDER:** You haven't told Sunny to begin with?

**RAYNIEDAY:** . . .

**SPIDER:** Um, don't you think you should?

**RAYNIEDAY:** No effing way. Cause, like, what if she tells Magnus and Slayer Inc.'s wrong and Mag and Maverick are best buddies? Then Magnus could go warn Maverick and I'll totally get nanoed. Then I'd definitely fail Trig—teacher sleepage or no.

**SPIDER:** I guess you've got a point.

**RAYNIEDAY:** No, I've got a stake, LOL.

**SPIDER:** Hehe. Okay, fine. Go slay some vamp butt. Good luck. I'm back from the graveyard, BTW. Rezzing now.

**RAYNIEDAY:** Uh, you might want to wait—

*\*\*Spider resurrects.*
*\*\*Shaman hits Spider for 975 damage.*
*\*\*Spider dies.*

**SPIDER:** NOOOOOO!!!!!

**RAYNIEDAY:** Sigh. And on that note, I'm logging. Got a busy day tomorrow. Evil vampires don't just slay themselves, you know.

POSTED BY RAYNE McDONALD @ 2:20 A.M.
THREE COMMENTS:

**DarkGothBoy says . . .**
You play World of Warcraft? Wow, you're such a cool chick. I'm on the Stonemaul server. Have a level 60 paladin. w00t! Are you into role-playing? We should totally cyber sometime.

**Rayne says . . .**
Um, remember that ten-foot pole thing? That counts for your virtual "lance" as well. Just. Not. Touching. Virtually or in real life. Get a life and stop reading my blog.

**Spider says . . .**
Jeez, Rayne, you had to put in the part about me dying? Couldn't you have cut and pasted that part out? Obviously it's so not relevant to this story and you make me look like a total nooblet in front of the WHOLE WORLD. And for the record, whole world people, I'm a really good player. It's just that Rayne sucks as a bodyguard. SUCKS, I tell you! It's so her fault that I'm always dead.

# 5

## The Blood Bar

I must be brief—I'm actually writing this from my BlackBerry from inside the Blood Bar!! Let me tell you, this place is creepy with a capital C! Or ghetto with a capital G. Or some kind of capital word for weird, sick, and twisted. (Which, I guess, would be three capital words: Weird, Sick, and Twisted, duh.)

First of all, I had to go through the total crackhead section of town. Wandering past pimps and prostitutes, drug dealers, and bums to find it. I half thought I'd get attacked and killed before I even got to my destination. Some slayer I'd turn out to be if I got myself killed by some punk mortal before I even got to stake my first vamp.

At least I look good. After all, one does not enter a vampire den unprepared and so I made a special effort to Goth things up even more than usual before I came. I've got on this black lacy corset top under my leather jacket, a black vinyl miniskirt, fishnets, and knee-high platform boots. The outfit, in conjunction with my overly blacked-out eyes, red lipstick and powered white face, makes me look pretty kick-ass, if you can excuse the vanity for a moment.

I find the address. A nondescript brick building. Which I guess makes sense. Obviously they're not going to have some neon sign out flashing "Get Sucked Here!" or anything. But this joint is beyond subtle. In fact, I'm not even sure if I have the right place—until a street-light glints on a tiny stained glass window embedded into the door . . . the shape of a drop of blood.

Bingo.

Not quite sure what to do, I knock. This big, burly bouncer type guy creaks opens the door from the other side and looks down at me with suspicious eyes. I meet his gaze, hopefully appearing less freaked out than I am. I mean, the dude looks like Vin Diesel if Vin Diesel took steroids. Yeah, that big. Except unlike the tanned action hero, this guy is pasty white. So, like a ghosty Vin Diesel on steroids. Which throws me a bit. Usually the vamp wanna-be crowd is all scrawny and lanky.

"What do you want?" he asks in a grumbly, growly voice.

Hm. Not exactly the rising star in the customer service department. Good thing I'm a slayer and not a secret shopper or I'd so be knocking off points already.

"I, um, am interested in being, uh . . ." Jeez, what's the correct terminology here? "Sucked?"

"I don't know what you're talking about."

I shake my head. Oh, so he's going to be like that, is he? "Yes, you do. You totally know. You're just pretending you don't because you're afraid I'm some cop or something. Well, I am not a cop. Obviously. I mean, since when do sixteen-year-olds become cops?"

"I don't think you're a cop. I think you're underage. We don't serve minors."

D'oh.

"Ha-ha." I laugh. "Did I say sixteen? Silly me. I meant twenty-one. Look, I even have an ID that proves it." I reach into my black canvas messenger bag and rummage through the front pocket for my wallet. Grabbing my fake ID, I present it to Vamp Diesel, hoping he won't notice my trembling hands.

"You're from Kentucky?" he asks, squinting at the photo (so not me). "And you're five eleven?"

"Only when I wear my stilettos."

He rolls his eyes, not looking all that convinced. "Run home and play with your dolls, um"—he glances at my ID—"Shaniqua." He snorts, handing me back my license. "This is not the place for you."

Okay, that's it. No more Miss Nice Rayne. I drop my eyes to the ground and flutter my lashes. Then I look up at him with my best Angelina Jolie imitation, pre–Brad Pitt/mommy era. "I don't play with dolls," I say, making my voice sultry and deep. "I play with vampires." I reach up and drag a lazy finger down the front of his massive chest. He stiffens immediately. Heh. Men are so easy.

"Well, I guess your license does say you're twenty-five. . . ." He hedges.

"I am twenty-five. Twenty-five and three quarters, to be exact." I smile coyly, reeling him in. "Now, please let me in. I'm *dying* to be sucked."

At first I'm not sure if he's going to go for this, but he surprises me by opening the door wide and gesturing me forward. I give him a little bow and step over the threshold.

"Fine, fine. But behave yourself," he instructs. "Don't make me sorry I let you in."

"I will," I promise. "I mean, I won't. Make you sorry, that is. I will behave. You won't even know I'm here. What's your name, anyway?"

"Francis. And I run the door most nights."

I rise onto my tiptoes to kiss his cheek. "Thank you, Francis," I say. "You won't regret this."

"I already do," he says, his face turning a slight pink color. Close as vamps get to blushing, I suppose. "But go in and have a good time before I change my mind."

I thank him once more, then head in. The door leads to a dark hallway, the walls painted with strange Celtic-looking designs that glow under the black lighting. Under my feet is a plush crimson rug. Weird, ambient mood music floats through the smoke-filled air. I guess the Blood Bar feels it's exempt from the no smoking laws of the rest of our state. Which makes sense, really, as lighting up is just where the sinning *starts* here.

The whole thing is truly spooky and I have half a mind to turn around and run back out the door screaming. But something compels me to keep moving forward. To see this through.

I reach the beaded curtain at the far side of the hallway and go through into the main bar. The place is decorated like a Valentine's Day card. Everything is red. Red velvet couches, red shag rugs, red walls, and red lightbulbs in the chandelier. The fuzzy lighting makes it hard to get a good look at the other patrons. Some are sprawled out on couches in a re-laxed, almost sleepy manner. Others are sitting on the edges of their seats, looking tense. All of them look like junkies— underfed, drawn faces, trembling hands.

This one guy standing over in the corner looks particularly foreboding. He appears fiftyish and is wearing a well-fitted black tux. Sandy-haired, high cheekbones, and an athletic physique, he has a sort of elegance about him that the other gaunt Blood Bar inhabitants lack. If I hadn't seen a photo of Maverick, I would have pegged this guy as the bar's owner, given the proprietary sense he exhibits as he surveys the lounge, arms crossed over his chest. But while he's definitely vampish, he's no Trent Reznor look-alike, so he can't be the big baddie we're here to find.

He catches me looking at him and gives me a small nod. Freaked out, I quickly drop my eyes. The last thing I need is to start drawing attention to myself.

"Do you have an appointment?" A sultry female voice behind me makes me turn around. A tall, voluptuous woman with long black hair to her waist has focused her huge violet eyes on me expectantly, a clipboard in her hands. She wears a crimson corset top and a long silky black skirt that's gotta be vintage or I'd so be asking her where she got it.

"I, um, do you take walk-ins here?" I stammer, caught off guard.

She frowns. "We certainly do not."

"Well, good. Because I, um, have an appointment." I squint down at her appointment book. Good thing I have excellent eyesight. "I'm Jane Smith."

She glances down at her clipboard. "Do you mean *James* Smith?"

Hm. Maybe time to see the eye doctor after all. "Yeah, that's me. James Smith. Evil parents really wanted a boy. Anyway, I go by Jane now. To my friends, anyway. Do you want to be my friend? I need more friends, actually. People to call me Jane."

She rolls her heavily made-up eyes. I know she doesn't believe me, but I've managed to annoy her enough that she just wants me out of her hair. Good strategy for dealing with teachers as well, by the way. Works every time.

"Fine, fine. James. Jane. Whatever. You're in room six." She gestures to the wall on the far side of the room. "Behind those curtains."

I swallow hard. This is it. I thank her and head to the back of the room, pulling aside the heavy velvet drapes. Behind it are ten nondescript doors, each with a gold number. I find room six and slip inside.

The room is dark, without any windows. The walls are painted black and thus suck out even the dim lighting given off by a few candles in the room. In the center is a big canopy bed with black linens. Even the floor has a charcoal-colored rug. Maybe they make it black so the bloodstains don't show as easily. The thought makes me a bit queasy and I close the door behind me and retreat to a wooden low-backed chair. What have I gotten myself into? This is totally Spooky World and I'm not just here for a visit.

Suddenly I realize the precariousness of my situation. I'm all alone in a vampire blood bar on the wrong side of town. And no one (besides Spider and I don't give Spider's rescue abilities much credit) knows where I am.

Some might call this a bad situation to be in. After all, I've got no plan. No idea what to do now that I'm here. What if I have to actually get sucked by some random gnarly vamp? What if I get some kind of awful disease? What if just sitting in here is infecting me?

Can we say Stupid, Rayne?

I take a deep breath, remembering what Mr. Teifert told me. The vamps here are all tested for diseases. I'm fine. I'm safe. From that, at least. And I have my stake, in case I meet with any danger. I reach into my bag, examine the chunk of unfinished wood, then sigh and put it away. Sadly, that *so* doesn't make me feel any more secure.

And that's where I am right about now. After forty-five minutes of waiting, my anxiety level has gone down and my boredom level has gone up. This is worse than the doctor's office. Nothing much to do. I've already checked my e-mail, played Tetris, chatted with Spider on IM. And now I'm writing my blog.

Oh, wait! Someone's coming. *Ooh*, this is it! More later.

**POSTED BY RAYNE McDONALD @ 8 P.M.**
**ONE COMMENT:**

**SunshineBaby says . . .**
Rayne! Are you just making this stuff up to see if I'm reading your blog? You're not really a slayer, are you? I mean, you'd come tell me if you were suddenly a slayer, right? You can't

keep something like that from your twin sister. Especially when the twin in question is dating a vampire. Which, I might add, is sort of your fault to begin with. Not to mention that the Blood Bar place sounds really dangerous. But I'm guessing this is just a joke to freak me out. I hope . . .

# 6

## Jareth

'm so getting my hair dyed black. Tomorrow. I'd do it to-night if I could find a drugstore that was still open. Just get a bottle of dye and dump it over my head. Something. Anything. Just so I don't look exactly like Sunny.

Sorry. Getting ahead of myself here.

So last I wrote I was in the Blood Bar, waiting for the vamp who's supposed to suck me, right? And it was a long wait, let me tell you. But finally the door opens.

The guy who enters the room is nothing like the other vamps I saw hanging out in the sitting room. The half-starved, junkie looking ones. This guy, while definitely a vamp with gorgeous fangage, is like a Jude Law clone. I know! Drool, right? Seriously, the dude's got the same dirty blond hair, same beautiful blue eyes (though his are rimmed with black eyeliner—yum!), and high cheekbones. He's tall. He's lanky. He's wearing a black wife-beater tank and tight black pants. His buff arms tell me he clocks in mucho time at the gym, but at the same time, he's simply tone, not bulky and meatheady like the bouncer, Francis, had been.

In other words, he's the most gorgeous Goth guy I've ever seen. And he's a vampire, too. Which automatically makes him not a poseur, like, uh, some of you. (Cough, cough, DarkGothBoy.)

Anyway, I'm all staring at him, totally and officially and instantly in love. I'm thinking, he can jump me, bite me, have his wicked way with me. Whatever his little black heart desires. He can take me on midnight strolls through ancient, ivy-walled cemeteries and kiss me senseless under the waning moon. Forget whiny, annoying Magnus. Sunny can have him. I want a blood mate like this guy.

"Hi, I'm Jareth, and I'll be your biter tonight," he mumbles in a deep, British-accented voice. OMG, yes! He's English, too! Major w00t! At this point I'm thinking this guy is way too good to be true. I wonder if he already has a blood mate, but I can't imagine he'd be working in a place like this, if he did. Maybe he's a lost soul, waiting for the love of a pure heart to redeem him like you always read about in those Christine Feehan books.

I watch intently as he wanders to the far side of the room, not yet glancing in my direction. He lazily sinks into the bed, extending his arms spread-eagle across the width of the pillows. His movements are slinky, almost catlike in their grace. He closes his beautiful sapphire eyes and smiles the most seductive smile known to mankind, his fangs slightly protruding from his mouth. Aha! Now we're talking.

I wonder if he's really as attractive as I think he is or if he's using the Vampire Scent on me. Vampires have this pheromone thing going on that makes them irresistible to humans. Probably how they rose to such power in this world. One grin and we're putty in their fangs.

"If you have any special requests, please tell me now and I'll do my best to accommodate you," he purrs in a throaty voice, shifting in the bed a bit, eyes still closed.

OMG, this guy oozes sex. He's practically dripping with it. I so want to jump him. Even more than I wanted to jump Ville when I went to see H.I.M. last fall. And that's saying something.

I shake my head. No, no, that will never do. One, this vamp's not really interested in me; it's his job to turn me on. I don't want to be like the fat guy who falls for the hooker. Two, he's one of the bad guys, duh. So even if he did—for some unfathomable reason—take an interest in me, I so can't start hooking up with one of Maverick's men. Then I'd have to war against my sister and her BF and that seems kind of lame. Not to mention I'd be nanovirused by Slayer Inc. A lousy situation all around.

"Um, hi, Jareth," I say, realizing he's waiting for an answer to his special requests question. Not that I can think of any. Well, not that I should say aloud anyway. Hm, maybe I should at least introduce myself. "Nice to meet you. I'm—"

"God!" Jareth interrupts as his eyes flutter open and he looks straight at me for the first time. Though with that accent, it comes out more like, "Gawd."

"Uh, no," I correct, though not unpleased at the idea. I like this guy's style. "I'm not God. At least I'm pretty sure I'm not. Though sometimes as a kid I used to pretend I was Aphrodite. You know, the goddess of love? But really, I'm just—"

"Your Majesty! What are you doing here?" he asks, scrambling off the bed and bowing low from the waist. "This is no place for you."

Oh-kay then. I stare at him, confused as all hell at this point. Is this some kind of weird role-playing they do here? Creepy. "Uh, no," I correct, "I'm not a queen or anything, either. I mean, sure, again, I wish. But really I'm just—"

"I know very well who you are, Majesty." His lips curl into a snarl, his blue eyes now a dark and stormy sea. He looks so angry. I take a cautionary step back. What have I gotten myself into? Does he know I work for Slayer Inc.? Is he going to alert the whole Blood Bar? Am I utterly screwed?

"Uh . . ." I manage, not at my most articulate.

Jareth grabs me by the shoulders, his nails digging into my skin, his gaze boring down on me. I'm shaking like crazy and am this close to bursting into tears. Some cool slayer chick I am. The way he's got me pinned I can't even whip out my stake. "Why did Magnus send you? Does he not trust me to get the job done?"

What? I look up at him, meeting his eyes for the first time. Did he just say "Magnus"?

"You know Magnus?" I ask, my voice totally croaky.

This could be bad. Very bad. Is my sister's boyfriend actually mixed up with the evils after all? Does this mean I have to slay him? Sunny will be so pissed if I slay her boyfriend, baddie or no. But then, I guess in the long run I'd be doing her a favor, right? Saving her from the Dark Side. Like when Luke killed his father, Darth Vader. Sort of. Okay, not really exactly the same.

He gives me a strange look. "Of course. I'm General Jareth of the Blood Coven Army. But you know that."

"I do?" I rack my brains. Then realization smacks me upside the head. Duh, duh, duh. "Oh! You think that I'm—"

"You know, I must say, I'm quite offended," Jareth rants, releasing my shoulders and running a hand through his hair. "I can't believe Magnus doesn't trust me. Sending his blood mate in to spy on me. And did he really think I wouldn't recognize you? After that night at Club Fang?"

"Dude, you have the wrong idea," I interrupt. "If you'd just calm down, I'll explain. I'm not Sunny. I'm—"

"Insulting. Unbearably insulting. I must go have a word with him this very second." Jareth pushes by me and heads out the door, slamming it behind him.

"I'm Rayne!" I cry after him. "Her sister."

He's so already gone.

I sigh, plopping down on the bed. These mistaken identity things really need to stop. First there was the whole Sunny getting my blood mate and almost becoming a creature of the night, now this. Definitely time to dye my hair black. Or develop an eating disorder like one of the Olsen twins. (Though that would force me to give up French fries.) But I have to do something. Anything to keep me from looking exactly like my sister.

Especially now that she's the Vampire Queen and I'm the slayer.

**POSTED BY RAYNE McDONALD @ 11 P.M.**
**FOUR COMMENTS:**

**ButterfliQT says . . .**
Wow, Rayne. I can't believe u went into that place by urself. Weren't you afraid they'd, like, kill u or something?

**Rayne says . . .**

Butterfli, we cannot all live our lives in fear. Some of us have destinies to fulfill. And, um, thanks for reminding me about the potential deathage. I really appreciate the support and encouragement. . . .

**Anonymous . . .**

Hey, Destiny Girl—you make yourself all high and mighty, but as far as I see it, you're still at square one. You haven't figured out anything about Maverick or his plans. You suck.

**Rayne says . . .**

First off, if you've got something to post in my blog, post it as yourself. Don't hide under anonymity. That's, like, way lame. Second off, this isn't some TV drama, where everything's solved in forty minutes between commercial breaks. Let's be realistic here. It's gonna take a few visits before I save the day. But never you fear, oh Anonymous One. I will succeed. After all, I am Rayne, The Vampire Slayer.

# 7

## Jareth the Jerk-Off

Quick entry before school as I didn't get to finish telling you the whole story last night. Was way too exhausted.

I leave the Blood Bar—not much more I can do tonight—and drive home. I'm exhausted at this point and just want to crawl in bed and get some shut-eye. But as I walk up the steps to the house, I hear a distinct *psst* coming from the bushes. I turn to look. It's my sister, Sunny, hiding in a bush.

I scrunch my eyebrows. "What are you—?"

She puts a finger to her lips and motions for me to follow. She leads me across the front lawn and to an elegant black stretch limo I hadn't noticed parked across the street. I climb inside after her and shut the door. The driver, obscured by a smoked-out glass window, pulls out.

I look around the limo. Whoa. Very elegant. Very vamp. The seats are crushed red velvet and there are crystal decanters filled with crimson liquid. Liquid I can almost guarantee is not some fine merlot.

Something inside of me aches a bit. You know, it's so not fair that this is Sunny's life and not mine. I did everything I was supposed to and now she's reaping all the rewards. I should have the riches, the powers, the gothed-out limo. The hot blood mate.

Speaking of, Magnus is sitting beside Sunny, all decked out in Armani as usual. I can see why she digs the guy. He looks just like Orlando Bloom in *Pirates of the Carribean*. Long black hair, pulled back, deep soulful eyes. (Though that might just be a trick of the light seeing as the guy has no soul. . . .)

I turn to my side and sigh when I see Jareth, the vamp from the Blood Bar, sitting next to me. Still dressed in his Goth best, a serious frown on his otherwise delish face. I sigh again. Great. He obviously sold me out. Sunny's going to be *sooo* pissed I didn't tell her the 411 about the whole slayer thing before heading out.

"What's going on, Rayne?" Sunny demands. Dressed in flip-flops, jeans, and tank top, she looks so out of place in the elegant, Gothic vampire limo. Annoys me to no end the fact that she now belongs here more than I do, let me tell you. At least they didn't fit her with a crown or something. Though I guess technically she's not Magnus's queen unless they get married, right? Can vampires even get married? I can't remember if that was covered in the training. I guess if they did it'd be more country club than church. . . .

Sorry. Digressing. I know.

"Uh, what do you mean?" I ask, not quite sure why I'm even attempting the innocent routine. There's no way she doesn't know.

"Jareth says he saw you down at the Blood Bar," Magnus clarifies. He has a sexy English accent, too. According to Sunny he was once a knight in shining armor for King Arthur in Camelot. I wonder if Jareth was as well. Not that I care.

"He assumed you were me," Sunny adds.

"Hm. I wonder why," I say sarcastically, still mad at him for scaring me so badly back at the bar. "Oh, wait. Could it be that he didn't shut up long enough to listen to one word I had to say? Could it be that he was too much in a hurry to run and go crying to Magnus before I even had a chance to explain?" I narrow my eyes and shoot daggers at Jareth. Jerk-off. Getting me in trouble with the vamps. So help me if this interferes with my position on the blood mate waiting list. "Thanks, dude, for selling me down the river. Two seconds and we could have cleared this whole thing up. But no. You had to *assume*. And you know what *assuming* does, don't you?" I elbow the vampire in the ribs. "Makes an 'ass' out of 'you' and 'me.' Or however that stupid phrase goes."

"I wouldn't mind you turning into an ass," Jareth growls in his throaty voice. "Then at least you couldn't speak."

"Oh yeah?" I cry, my blood boiling at this point. I'm, like, this close to smacking the guy upside the head. Or whipping out my stake, even. That'd show him. No one should be able to talk to me like that and live. "Well . . . then I could, um, bray, and I bet that would be even more annoying."

"I'd take my chances."

"Jareth! Rayne!" Magnus scolds. "This childish bickering is not helping us get to the bottom of this."

"You're right," I agree. Then when Magnus isn't looking I stick my tongue out at Jareth. He scowls back at me. OMG, what a loser, right? And that "ass" comment was completely uncalled for. Especially since back at the Blood Bar he wouldn't let me get a word in edgewise while he ranted and raved and pulled out his hair. I take everything back about him being a sexy guy I'd want to have vampire babies with.

"Why were you at the Blood Bar, Rayne?" Sunny asks, her voice all concerned and big sister like. Technically though, I'm the older one. By seven whole minutes. Just cause she's dating some guy who's, like, a thousand years old doesn't mean suddenly she's more wise and mature. "And that thing in your blog? About being a vampire slayer? Was that just a joke? Cause if that was a joke, it wasn't very funny."

Oh, I see. NOW she reads my blog. Now that she's back to being a human and it makes no difference whatsoever. I begged her to read the thing when she was about to turn vampire. As you know, it has a ton of important info about the process. But no! She had better things to do. Like make out with her cheeseball prom date Jake Wilder.

I swallow hard. Explanation time.

"It's not a joke. Your drama coach, Mr. Teifert, is really vice prez of Slayer Inc. And he's tagged me as the next slayer." I lean back in my seat, crossing my left leg over my right, somewhat enjoying the shocked looks on everyone's faces. Especially Jareth's. Heh. I bet he wishes he didn't make enemies with me now. Now that he knows how dangerous I can be. One wrong move and BAM! Stake that!

"Why would he pick you?" Sunny asks, the first to recover her voice.

I shrug. "I don't know. He was all saying it's my destiny or something."

"Can't you just refuse?"

"That's the messed up part," I admit. "He claims he's put some nanovirus in my bloodstream that will be activated if I refuse to perform my slayerly duties. I don't know if it's true or not, but I don't want to take any chances, you know?"

"Nano what?" Sunny asks, scrunching up her freckled nose. "That's crazy. He's got to be pulling your leg. Maybe he overheard us talking and . . ."

"I'm afraid not, Sunny," Magnus says, reaching over to put a slender white hand on her knee. My virginal twin squirms a bit under his touch. She wants him, I can tell, but she's fighting the run to second base. I wonder how long it will take Maggy to score that first home run. "That's Slayer Inc.'s typical MO. They have operatives in every major hospital who tag infants in the maternity ward who they deem to be potential slayers."

Ugh. So the nano thing probably is true. Great. I was so hoping Mag would laugh it off and tell me Slayer Inc. had no real hold on me. Evidently not so much.

"But Rayne can't kill vampires!" Sunny interjects. "I mean, she wants to be one! And . . . and what if she has to kill you?" My twin looks close to tears at this point. She had a run-in with Bertha, the old slayer, once upon a time and it scarred her for life.

"You know, you're going to score lousy on the reading comprehension part of the MCATs," I say. "You obviously only skimmed my blog entry."

"Well, I'm sorry. My twin sister announces to the world that she's the next Buffy. I'm supposed to spend time reading between the lines?"

"Listen, Sun," I assure her, trying to play nice. "They only want me to kill the bad vampires. Not the ones who coexist peacefully with humanity. For example, Magnus here. He's one of the good guys. So I'd never be asked to slay him."

"Oh." Sunny sniffs, still frowning in bewilderment. "Well,

that's good, I guess." She glances over at Magnus. He smiles at her and reaches over to brush a lock of hair from her eyes, then kisses her softly. Bleh. Enough with the PDA. I steal a glance over at Jareth. He's staring out the window doing the brooding thing.

"Um, anyway," I say, clearing my throat. "They've asked me to go undercover in the Blood Bar. I'm supposed to do recon on this baddie vamp called Maverick. Evidently he's up to no good. Wants to do something takeoverish to Magnus here. So actually, I'm helping the cause."

"Well, there's no need for that," Jareth butts in, turning back from window stareage. "I have 'the cause,' as you call it, completely under control. I certainly do not need assistance from an operative of Slayer Inc."

Oh, right. Of course he doesn't. After all, he was doing such a fine job on his own this evening, what with running out of the Blood Bar practically screaming simply 'cause he met a girl that looked like his boss's GF.

"Let's not be so hasty, Jareth," Magnus says slowly. "Perhaps Rayne can be of some use."

"Yeah," I say, making a "nyah, nyah" face at Jareth. "I'm very . . . useful."

"I can't imagine," Jareth mutters.

God, I've never met such an arrogant, pain in the butt vamp in all my sixteen years. Not that I've met boatloads or anything, but still.

"Here, as Sunny would say, is the 411," Magnus interjects, and I chuckle, despite myself. It so sounds funny to hear a former knight in shining armor, now Master of the Vamps, use twenty-first-century slang. "Slayer Inc. is not the only group concerned about Maverick's extracurricular activities. I, too, have gotten intelligence that leads me to believe that he has some kind of plan brewing as well. I've sent Jareth in undercover to do some reconnaissance. That's why you met him in the bar. He was working for me."

"And it was all going very well before *she* came along," Jareth mutters under his breath.

"Uh, hello?" I say, waving my hands in his face. "The 'she' in this scenario is sitting next to you!" I am so not going to take his BS.

"Jareth, I know you're frustrated because you lost a night of recon due to Rayne's appearance," Magnus says, staving off Jareth's retort before it can leave his lips. "But I think if we look at the long-term situation, this could actually work out in our favor. As a human, Rayne will be given a different view of the Blood Bar. Between the two of you, we can probably get a very decent picture of what's going on down there. I think you should work together."

I raise my eyebrows. Hold on one gosh-darn second. Work together? Magnus wants me to work together with this guy? Bleh.

I glance over at Jareth, who looks even less pleased at the idea than I am.

"I can't work with . . . the slayer!" he cries, spitting out the job title as if it were poison. "Never in a million years." He looks to Magnus, his piercing blue eyes pleading. "I can do this myself, Your Majesty. I am your general. I command your army. I don't need some high school kid tagging along. She'll only get in the way."

"Rayne is more than just a high school student. She's the first slayer in a thousand years to have gone through all the vampire training. To have an insider's look into our world."

"But—"

"This could be the beginning of a great partnership between Slayer Inc. and our kind," Magnus continues. "I'm not going to ruin that opportunity because of your personal hang-ups. I'm sorry about what happened, Jareth. But that was long ago. If we are to survive as a species, we must learn to adapt. Rayne can be helpful to you. And I expect you to accept her help."

"Never!" Jareth growls. "I will never accept the help of a slayer. Magnus, you are a fool if you trust them. Look what happened the last time. And look what they did to Lucifent." The limo pulls up at a red light and Jareth reaches for the door handle. "I am overdue for my feeding," he says, as if that's really the reason he's bailing. Before anyone has a chance to speak, he's out the door and into the night.

I lean back in my seat, pressing my head against the leather interior. Suddenly I'm very tired. And I'm not entirely sure I know what's going on. This slayer stuff is still pretty new. And now we've thrown an unwilling vampire in the mix. Super.

"Don't worry," Magnus says. "Jareth can be pigheaded at times, but he's a fine solider. A professional. He'll come around."

"Cool," I say with absolutely no enthusiasm. "Can't wait to be coworkers with the guy."

**POSTED BY RAYNE McDONALD @ 10 a.m.**
**TWO COMMENTS:**

**Angelbaby3234566 says . . .**
If u ask me, that Jareth guy sounds like a big baby. What's his deal anyway? He should be honored to work with u! U rox!

**DarkGothBoy says . . .**
See? He'd rather jump out of a speeding limo then spend time with you. I told you the slayer thing would screw with your love life. Shoulda hooked up with me when you had a chance, Slayer Girl.

**Soulsearcher says . . .**

Obviously this Jareth guy's got issues. I wonder what he has against slayers? You think he's got some deep, dark, painful secret? I just love vampires with deep, dark, painful secrets. Maybe you'll be the one girl who can redeem his lost, tortured soul and the two of you will fall desperately in love and live eternity as a holy bonded pair. (Insert dreamy sigh here.)

**Rayne says . . .**

Oh yeah, deep, dark, painful secrets are SUCH a turn-on. But no, I just think Jareth is a big, arrogant loser. And he'd probably rather start dating a Chihuahua than have me redeem his lost, tortured soul.

# 8

## OMG!

O MG, OMG, OMG! I just got some news that will totally blow you away! I'm so freaking out I can barely type. And that's saying something.

It all came about after Sunny IMed me from her room across the hall. Transcript of convo is as follows:

**SUNSHINEBABY:** Hey, you awake?

**RAYNIEDAY:** Yeah. Just finishing up playing videogames with Spider.

**SUNSHINEBABY:** Ah. You and your gaming. You're such a geek.

**RAYNIEDAY:** And this is from a girl who likes Dave Matthews.

**SUNSHINEBABY:** How many times do I have to tell you? It's normal to like Dave Matthews.

**RAYNIEDAY:** If you say so, geek.

**SUNSHINEBABY:** Sigh. Anyway . . .

**RAYNIEDAY:** Yes. What's up?

**SUNSHINEBABY:** Nothing. Just wanted to say sorry for going all ambushy on you earlier, but when Jareth came to Mag he was totally freaking out. So Mag figured it'd be better to just all sit down and work this all out ASAP.

**RAYNIEDAY:** Yeah, that's cool. I'm all for that. Don't know about Jareth though.

**SUNSHINEBABY:** Yeah, totally. I wonder what his deal is.

**RAYNIEDAY:** You didn't ask Magnus?

**SUNSHINEBABY:** I tried, but he just said basically that Jareth has intimacy issues.

**RAYNIEDAY:** Don't we all.

**SUNSHINEBABY:** LOL.

**RAYNIEDAY:** It's too bad he's such a jerk. He's super hot. Totally blood mate material. Unless he already has one.

**SUNSHINEBABY:** No, according to Magnus, Jareth has always refused to accept a blood mate.

**RAYNIEDAY:** Really? I thought that was what all vamps wanted. Waited a thousand years to have.

**SUNSHINEBABY:** Shrug. Dunno. Evidently not Jareth.

**RAYNIEDAY:** I bet something really terrible happened to him. Like really, really bad. Maybe even by a slayer. Maybe he had a blood mate before and the slayer whacked her. His heart was broken and he swore he'd never love again.

**SUNSHINEBABY:** Yeah. That'd be soooo romantic.

**RAYNIEDAY:** Or he could just be an a-hole. Like Dad.

**SUNSHINEBABY:** Ohhhh!!!

**RAYNIEDAY:** ?

**SUNSHINEBABY:** I totally forgot to tell you!!!!!

**RAYNIEDAY:** . . .

**SUNSHINEBABY:** Dad's coming!

**RAYNIEDAY:** What the hell are you talking about?

**SUNSHINEBABY:** For our birthday! Dad's coming for our birthday!

**RAYNIEDAY:** Yeah, right.

**SUNSHINEBABY:** No. I'm serious. I e-mailed him last week and asked him if he'd come to our birthday party. And he wrote back yesterday afternoon. Then the whole Blood Bar Jareth thing went down and I totally forgot until just now.

Okay, time out on the IM transcript to give you a little 411 on the 'rents and the Dad situation. You see, our mom spent her formative teen years in New York City, during the 1970s. Which means she should have been all into disco, Studio 54, and glittery nightwear, right? Partying it up, doing lots of speed, having sex with strangers. Whatever those disco divas used to do. But no. Not my mom. My mom decided to leave the city to head out to this commune upstate. A place where they wore woven clothing and milked cows and sheared sheep. I'm still thinking there were heavy drugs involved to make her want to get up close and personal to smelly, hairy barnyard animals, but probably more the hallucinatory hippie dippy drugs rather than coke or something.

Anyway, at the commune she met my dad. He was trying to "find himself" even then. And he thought a beautiful, blond and barefoot hippie like my mom would be just the ticket to his happiness. He wooed her off the farm, bought her a house in the Massachusetts suburbs, and knocked her up with twins. My mom totally worshiped the ground he walked on, even though mostly he spent his time walking all over her.

About four years ago, he told Mom he felt "trapped" and he needed time to "find himself." At first, I kind of understood. After all, our town is pretty dull. But I became a little doubtful of this pilgrimage to self-realization when I learned the method of travel was a brand-new red Corvette; his Mecca was evidently the holy city of Las Vegas; and his secretary, Candi, was along for the ride.

We haven't seen him since. Not that I've wanted to. In fact, up until now I've always said I'd sooner join the cheerleading squad and go out with quarterback Mike Stevens than bond with dear old Dad. And that's saying something.

**RAYNIEDAY:** So let me get this straight. You e-mailed Dad?

**SUNSHINEBABY:** ☺

**RAYNIEDAY:** And you asked him to our birthday party?

**SUNSHINEBABY:** Yup, yup.

**RAYNIEDAY:** And he said . . . YES?!?!?

**SUNSHINEBABY:** Isn't that awesome? I'm so excited I can hardly stand it.

**RAYNIEDAY:** I can't believe he said yes. He never comes to these kinds of things. We haven't seen him in years. Are you SURE he said yes?

**SUNSHINEBABY:** I'll forward you the e-mail. Hold on. . . .

---

To: SunshineBaby@yours.com
From: RMcDonald@vegasbaby.com

Hiya kiddo,

Great to hear from you. Sounds like you're doing well in school. Congrats on your role in the senior class play. Maybe you'll be the next Lindsay Lohan.

I can't believe you two are turning seventeen. I remember when you were tiny screaming babies running around in diapers. How time flies.

Anyway, I just checked my Day-Timer and it doesn't look like anything's going on the weekend of your party. And I was able to find a cheap flight on JetBlue. So count me in!

I'll even bring the birthday cake. There's a bakery down the street from me that's to die for.

Thanks again for thinking of me.
Love,
Dad

---

**RAYNIEDAY:** Wow. I can't believe it. I don't know what to say.

**SUNSHINEBABY:** I know. Me neither. I just sent the e-mail figuring that it'd guilt him a bit into remembering he had daughters that he never communicated with. I never in a billion years thought he would actually say yes and come.

**RAYNIEDAY:** He could still blow us off. . . .

**SUNSHINEBABY:** No way. He bought a plane ticket and e-mailed me the itinerary. And he rented a hotel room downtown. He's definitely coming.

**RAYNIEDAY:** Wow. I can't believe it.

Anyway, the chatting goes on, but that's the important bit. Sunny ends up signing off to go to bed and I go back to writing this new blog entry. It's a bit hard to type, even now, what with my hands all trembly from the news.

Dad. Coming here. For our birthday. A combination of dream come true and scary nightmare. I wonder what he'll be like. If he'll have gotten fat or bald. If he still has that ticklish spot behind his right ear. If his favorite food is still mac and cheese. If it'll be like he never left or if it'll be weird and awkward. Will he remember all our inside jokes? The stories he used to tell us?

The storytelling is the best part about Dad. Sunny and I would curl up in my parents' big king-size bed, each resting our heads on one of his shoulders. He'd spin fantastical tales. Fantasy, horror, comedy, adventure. Every night he'd have a different story, but the heroines were always the same. Two princesses, Sunshine and Rayne, who went about saving the world. Even when I got too old for those kinds of stories, I'd always beg for more.

Back then Dad was my superhero. My idol. The person I wanted to be like when I grew up. He was so cool. And he understood me in a way that Mom and Sunny never could. Him and I used to sit out on the back porch on warm summer nights and have deep discussions about life, the universe, and everything.

And then one day he left. Breaking my heart in the process.

The shrinks tell Mom that's why I am like I am today. Keeping myself at arm's length from people, not trusting anyone to get close. Dressing rebelliously. Having seedy flings with boys I don't care about and then walking out on them before they know what happened.

The question is this: Could Dad be to blame for all of it or was I always destined to be a freak? Guess I'll never know for sure.

Wow. I can't believe he's actually coming next week.
That he's flying on a plane. Staying at a hotel.
That he's bringing birthday cake.
Okay, I am officially freaking out.


**POSTED BY RAYNE McDONALD @ 11 P.M.**
**ONE COMMENT:**


**Ashleigh says...**
That's so kewl ur dad is coming 2 visit. I haven't seen my dad
in like 10 years, so I totally know the feeling.


~~**Anonymous says...**~~
~~Ooh, little Raynie has Daddy issues. No wonder you've
turned out such a LOSER.~~
**COMMENT DELETED BY BLOG ADMINISTRATOR**

# 9

## Black Is the New Black

So want to hear the good news or the bad news?

Oh, forget it. I hate when people ask that stupid question, anyway. It's not like they really want you to choose. They've already got a preferred news-telling order in their heads. They're just trying to prepare you for the shock/horror of the bad news which is ALWAYS in these cases worse than the good news.

Examples:

**GOOD NEWS:** You got an "A" on your history paper.
**BAD NEWS:** You have to read it aloud in class.

**GOOD NEWS:** The Arctic Monkeys are coming to town.
**BAD NEWS:** It's a twenty-one and up show and last week some bar confiscated your fake ID.

**GOOD NEWS:** There's a sale at Hot Topic.
**BAD NEWS:** It's only on candy-colored big pants rave gear, not that amazingly cool red velvet corset you've been eyeing.

ANYWAY, my good news is that I did it. I went and dyed my hair black. This beautiful ebony color that's so dark and rich it looks almost blue. Now no one will ever mistake me for Sunny in three billion years.

Cheer!

Bad news? Uh, Mom totally flipped when she saw it.

"What did you do to yourself?" she cries when I walk out of the bathroom. (Yes, it was a "do-it-yourself" project—I'm not spending $100 at the hairdresser when they sell the stuff in the drugstore for $8.99.)

"I dyed my hair black," I reply, though I'm pretty sure it was a rhetorical question on her part.

She grabs a chunk of hair, her expression as distraught as when I told her I had pierced my tongue last year. "But you had beautiful blond hair. Why would you do this?"

"Mom, I'm sick of looking exactly like Sunny," I say.

"Everyone keeps mistaking me for her and it's getting annoying."

"How can people mistake you two? You dress completely differently," she says, gesturing to my current ensemble of black on black on black.

"I don't know." I shrug. "I agree my superior taste in clothing should tip them off, but evidently not so much. I'm an individual, Mom. I'm my own person. I need to express myself."

"No, you need to obey me. That's what you need to do," Mom returns. Her hazel eyes flash fire. Wow. I haven't seen her this mad since Sunny went vamp and started missing curfew on a regular basis. (Which is SUCH a bigger deal than a little Clairol #70, IMO.) "And you know very well I don't want you dyeing your hair."

"But, Mom—"

"Do you know what kinds of chemicals they put in those dyes?" she demands, hands on hips. "Stuff that can cause cancer in lab rats. And if it can cause cancer in lab rats, what do you think it can do to you?"

I groan. I should have guessed that she didn't really care about the look. After all, she's a pretty unconventional dresser herself. No, my mom doesn't worry about what the PTA will say. She's too wrapped up in her government conspiracy theories in which Men in Black are developing evil hair dye to sedate the human race while the Illuminati take over the world.

Sometimes I wish I just had a normal mom. One who didn't think hairdressers were really the Antichrist, at the very least.

"I'm sorry, Mom. I guess I wasn't thinking."

"Come to me next time if you want to change your look. I've got a great all-natural henna coloring we could have used. Stuff that's made of plant products and is perfectly safe."

"Sure, Mom. I will." Yeah, right. I'm so not getting my hair dyed with henna. Maybe I'd consider a henna tattoo, but that's where I draw the line. After all, let's face it. Safe and effective or not, henna is for hippies.

She reaches over and gives me a hug. "I'm sorry, Rayne," she says. "I don't mean to yell. I just worry about my girls. I want them to be safe."

"I know, Mom. And I'm glad you do," I say, squeezing her back.

I mean it, too. Though she drives me crazy at times, overall when it comes to moms, mine's about as cool as you can get. She's like a "friend mom." Sunny and I can talk to her about pretty much anything (besides hair dye and vampires, of course) and she's completely nonjudgmental. She doesn't sneak into our rooms and read our diaries or go on MySpace to make sure our profiles are appropriate. (I'm RaynieDay,

BTW, if anyone wants to friend me.) My friend Ashleigh's mom grounded her for like four weeks when she found out Ashleigh had posted sexy pics of herself on MySpace. Not that I have any sexy pics posted, just FYI. (Sorry DarkGothBoy.)

So yeah, she's okay. If not a little overprotective at times.

After we pull away from the hug, I notice something surprising. "Hey, Mom, what's up with your outfit?"

Wow. The woman who LIVES in bell-bottom jeans or long flowered skirts and peasant blouses is currently standing in front of me wearing a sexy little black dress with high heels and a pearl necklace. I can't believe I'm just noticing it now. Observe much, Rayne?

"Oh, this old thing?" she asks, blushing furiously as she smoothes the front of the dress. "I've had it for years."

"Just FYI, that'd be much more believable if you'd removed the price tag," I suggest, gesturing to her sleeve.

"Oh." The blush deepens as she reaches to rip off the tag in question. "I guess I've just never worn it."

Eesh. The woman is the worst liar in the known universe. "Spill, Mom."

She sighs and motions for me to come into her bedroom. I follow, plopping down on the old-fashioned, four-poster bed that Grandma left when she died. It would be an elegant piece of furniture if Mom hadn't covered it with a Technicolor-hand-stitched quilt from her commune days. Still, I've got to admit, overall the room is pretty cozy and homey. When

Sunny and I were little and big thunderous storms would crash through our neighborhood, we always ran to the oversized bed, crawling under the covers with Mom and Dad. Only then did we feel warm and safe.

Um, anyway . . .

So Mom shuts the door behind us and joins me on the bed. She tries to pull her feet up and under like normal, then realizes she has a nice dress on and chooses to cross her ankles daintily instead. I have to bite my lip not to laugh.

"So?" I prod.

"So . . . I've got a date," she whispers, her eyes alight with mischievous excitement. She's totally forgotten that she's pissed at me about my hair.

"A date?" I cry. "That's awesome!"

She studies me, her gaze turning motherly. "Are you sure? I mean, I know that's got to seem a little weird. Your mom dating someone."

"No! It's not weird at all. I think it's great." After all, I've been dying for the woman to get out of the house for years. Pining away in a nunlike existence—hoping the next time the door opens my dad will walk through—is just not a way for someone to live. Even a mom. "So who's the lucky guy? Where did you meet him?"

I wonder for a moment if I should tell her about Dad coming to the b-day party, but decide not to rain on her parade just yet. We've got nearly a week to break the news and I don't want to ruin her big date.

Her cheeks pinken. It's adorable. I love seeing her so excited. "Actually I bumped into him at the harvest co-op last night," she says. "Literally. We were both reaching for the same frozen chickpea burgers."

I smile. Obviously love at first sight. With the only other person in the known universe who would actually eat a chickpea burger. "Very nice. And he asked you out?"

"Yeah, we're going for dinner at Abe and Louis in Boston."

I whistle. "Fan-cy."

She giggles. I haven't seen her like this in years. Maybe in forever. I love it.

"Where's this guy from? What's he do for a living?" I ask.

She shrugs. "I didn't interrogate him in the frozen foods section, Rayne."

"Right. Well, definitely find out all the 411 tonight," I say, mothering my mother. "We want to make sure he's the right guy for you. We can't have you going out with just anyone."

She laughs. "Okay, dear. I promise I'll get you the full scoop."

At that moment the doorbell chimes. My mom jumps off the bed and is at the door in a flash. "That must be him," she says, looking back at me with a grin. "Wish me luck!"

I hold up crossed fingers. "Luck!"

She scurries downstairs and I take the opportunity to peek out her window, which offers a good front porch view. There's a guy at the door—dressed in a tux, no less. I can't make out his face, but he seems well built, with a full head of hair. Not hippielike at all, either, which is probably for the best. And the coolest part? He arrived in a limo. Crazy.

Anyway—Mom on a date, and me off the hook for my hair-coloring experiment. Time to head to the Blood Bar and save the world.

**POSTED BY RAYNE McDONALD @ 8 P.M.**
**FOUR COMMENTS:**

**Spider says . . .**
Ooh, Rayne—I can't WAIT to see ur new hair. You gotta take a camera phone pic and send it 2 me ASAP! And your mom on a date? Whoa!

**SunshineBaby says . . .**
Mom's on a date? A date? You let her take off with some strange guy without even meeting him first? What if he's some psycho killer? Wasn't there one in the news the other day? And did they catch him? I don't think they caught him, Rayne! OMG! Mom could be dating the psycho killer right now.

If she's not home by eleven, I'm so calling the police. Or

maybe by ten. Gah! She needs to start carrying a cell phone so we can check in with her. I can't BELIEVE you let her go.

**Ashleigh says . . .**
Your mom is way cooler than mine, Rayne. I still can't believe my mom grounded me over my MySpace profile. I mean, puh-leeze. The pics weren't even that bad. It wasn't like I was naked or anything. Just hot. But she's all, like, "Oh, the perverted old men are gonna see them." Like I'm going to friend some perverted old man. What-EVER. Anyway, now I'm on Facebook instead and she has no idea. Sweet!!!

**DarkGothBoy says . . .**
You don't have to post sexy pics on MySpace, baby. Just e-mail them directly to me. Or better yet, how about you come over and I'll take some pics for you? I got a new digital camera for my birthday and I'm dying to try it out. And, oh? Don't you feel like a loser? Your mom is getting more action than you are. Tsk, tsk.

# 10

## Bite Me, Bay-Bee!

I've got to stop with these late nights. They're totally killing me at school. Today (or yesterday, if you consider it's once again past midnight) I slept through Algebra II, American History, and three quarters of Art. (*Sooo* embarrassing to wake up facedown in a palette of paint. Took me a half hour to scrub the stuff off.)

Being a slayer is like having a second full-time job. Luckily I'm not really a homework girl to begin with or I'd be so screwed.

But enough about boring old school. You guys want to hear about the Blood Bar, right? Of course you do.

So I wait 'til after dark and then head on over. My buddy

Vin Vamp (a.k.a. Francis) is back on the door tonight, which is a total relief. I so didn't want to have to whip out my painfully bad fake ID again and try to act all convincing.

"Hey, Frannie," I greet. "How's the biting?"

"You're back," he observes, folding his massive arms across his chest and staring at me with cool eyes. "Couldn't stay away, eh?"

"Nope! You know me," I say playfully, punching him lightly on the arm. "Well, actually you don't, I guess. But you will. Soon. I plan on becoming a regular. You'll see me every night. We can develop clever nicknames for each other and banter a while before you let me in."

"*If* I let you in."

"See? Banter." I smile sweetly. "We're well on our way to a beautiful friendship already."

Francis tries to hide his smile without much luck. He totally thinks I'm adorable, I can tell. "You know, Shaniqua," he says, still calling me by my fake ID name, "you're really a piece of work." He shakes his head. "Okay, okay. Come on in." He pulls open the door and gestures inside.

But something makes me pause at the door. I look up at Francis's face, studying it closer. While he does seem amused, there's something about his smile. Like it doesn't quite meet his eyes. And I don't mean in some secretly nefarious, up-to-no-good, one-of-the-bad guys way.

He just looks . . . a bit sad.

"What's wrong, Frannie?" I ask. "No offense or anything, but you look like someone just ran over your pet bat."

Francis rubs his bald head with the palm of his hand. He really is a big oafy looking dude for a vampire. "My blood mate is missing," he confesses. "If you must know. And I'm worried sick about her."

I've explained the blood mate thing, right? Well to recap real quick, each vamp, once they hit a thousand years old, gets to turn one willing human into a vampire. They do all this complex DNA testing beforehand to make sure the human and vamp will be compatible. 'Cause after all, they're destined to be together for all eternity, so you want to make sure it's a good match. For example, I was matched up with Magnus originally, before he bit Sunny by mistake. Luckily twins share DNA so those two were still compatible.

Bottom line, a blood mate is sort of like a soul mate, except without that whole messy soul part. So needless to say, the two vamps are usually attached at the hip. Like an immortal BF/GF with no way to ever divorce.

"I'm sorry to hear that," I say, genuinely feeling bad for the guy. I mean, that sucks, right? What if his blood mate met a new vamp and took off to Vegas, like Dad did? Leaving poor Frannie here all alone in the world with major trust issues.

Francis kicks the ground with his toe. Let me tell you, the guy's feet make Michael Jordan look like a midget. I'd hate to meet him in a back alleyway.

Oh, wait, we're in a back alleyway. Uh, never mind.

"Her name is Dana. She works here as a biter," Francis explains.

Of course, I'm all wondering if a bouncer dating a biter is as cliché as a bouncer dating a stripper. But Frannie looks so upset, I decide not to ask. And really, who am I to judge?

"Three days ago, she called in sick. And she hasn't shown up since. She's not been back to the crypt. In fact, I've searched everywhere for her. It's like she's dropped off the face of the earth."

"I'm sure she'll turn up," I say, trying to sound comforting. I pat him on his big hairy forearm. "Don't worry."

He grins ruefully and pats me on the head. "Thanks," he says. "You're probably right. Nothing to be concerned over." He gestures to the door. "Would you like to go in?"

"Please."

I walk inside, once again enveloped by the dim lighting, smoky air, and crimson interiors, this time soundtracked by the band She Wants Revenge, crooning from some hidden overhead speakers. I can't say I'm surprised to learn that vamps dig Emo.

I enter the lounge and approach the hostess.

"Hey, I'm back," I say, trying to act as nonchalant as possible. "Can I get the same biter as yesterday? Jareth, I think his name was? He was uber hot."

I giggle to myself as she checks the list. Jareth's going to be so annoyed when he sees me again. But, hey, I'm just simply following orders. If he has a problem with me, he'll have to take it up with Magnus.

"Sure. He's not with anyone at the moment," the hostess says. "Go ahead to room six and I'll send him in."

Perfect. I thank the woman and head behind the curtain to room six, praying that Jareth doesn't take forty-five minutes to show up this time. I forgot my Game Boy DS and I'm so not the type of girl who can just sit around and twiddle her thumbs contentedly. Besides, we've got a mission to accomplish here. No time for goofing around.

Luckily it only takes about five minutes for the door to open and "Hotness" to walk through.

"Hi, my name is Jareth, and I'll be your— God!" He curses as he lays his eyes on me.

I raise an eyebrow. "You'll be my god? Hm . . . Well, we'll have to see about that. I mean, it takes a lot to rock my world these days."

His powder-white face pinkens and he quickly changes the subject. Heh. "What the hell are you doing here?" he growls. "I thought I told you I work alone."

"And I thought I told you I don't listen to stupid, pig-headed vampires. And if I didn't, well consider this fair warning."

"Watch out, little girl," Jareth says, looming over me, raising his arms in what I assume he means to be a threatening, evil gesture. "I am a creature of the night. I am not to be toyed with."

I roll my eyes. "Ooh. I'm scared."

He lowers his hands and huffs in annoyance. "Well, you bloody well should be. I could bite you, you know."

"And I could stake you," I say, rummaging through my messenger bag to pull out the chunk of wood Teifert gave me. I stand up and wave it at Jareth's face. "One false move and . . . POW!"

Jareth stares at the stake, then at me, then back to the stake. Then, to my surprise, he bursts out laughing.

"What?" I scowl, so not appreciating his reaction. After all, I am a vampire slayer, right? He should be shaking in his boots just at the mere sight of me.

"What . . . the hell . . . is that?" he asks, between chortles. He's laughing so hard he's holding his stomach.

"A stake."

"That's not a stake. It's a chunk of wood."

"Well, it's . . . not . . . finished yet," I say, defensively, lowering the weapon. "I need to carve it. Embed it with my own essence." Wow, that sounds a lot dumber when it comes out of my mouth.

"Bwahahahaha!" Jareth continues laughing at my expense. "What are you going to do? Give the evil vampires splinters?"

I can feel my face heat with embarrassment, which is *sooo* annoying. How dare he make fun of me? I have been put on this earth to slay his kind. One false move and I'll go all destiny on his ass.

Somehow. Though probably not with this particular stake. . . .

Grrr . . .

"Shut up!" I cry, unable to come up with one of my infamous Rayne comebacks. "Stop laughing at me."

Jareth sighs, reaching up to wipe the bloody tears of mirth from his eyes. "Oh, Rayne," he says, shaking his head. "You're precious, you know that?"

"Well, you're just lame and annoying." Why does it seem like I've totally lost the banter battle here?

Jareth holds out his hand. "Give me the stake."

Oh, yeah, right. Like I'm going to fall for that one. It may not be finished, but it's the only weapon I've got. I hide it behind my back.

"No effing way."

Jareth sighs. "Just for a minute."

"Why? So you can render me completely defenseless and suck me dry?"

"With that as your weapon, you already are completely defenseless, sweetie."

I sigh. I know he's right. Reluctantly I hand over the stake. Stupid Slayer Inc. for giving me such a pathetic weapon. After all, Buffy the Vampire Slayer got swords and axes and crossbows. Is that so much to ask for?

Jareth turns the stake around in his hands. Then he reaches into his pocket and pulls out a Swiss Army knife. I involuntarily jump back.

"Relax," he says. "I'm going to help you carve."

He clicks open the blade and starts running it across the wood, shaving off chunks. I watch, mesmerized, as a pretty nice stake emerges from the mess.

"I am a sculptor by trade," he explains. "Mostly my carvings are of stone, but the principle is the same." He hands me the stick and knife. "Now you try. Run the blade down, away from you."

I do as he instructs, slicing into the wood.

"No. Like this." He comes around behind me and takes my hands in his and guides me through the next stroke. "There you go," he says in my ear.

Now, for the record, I must repeat here that he is, without a doubt, the most annoying vampire in the known universe and I can't stand him. In fact, if they said he was the last blood mate on earth, I'd choose to remain human just to stay away from him. If he was the last man on earth, I'd turn lesbian. If he was the last person on earth, I'd become a nun.

That said, he really is freaking HOT. And when I feel his cool breath in my ear as he helps me carve, my body totally betrays me and gets all mushy inside. Which is so frustrating! Gah!

"Okay, I, um, think I've got it now," I say, desperate for

him to take a step back before I do something really stupid, like turn around and kiss him. "Thanks."

To my relief (and disappointment if I'm being totally honest here) he lets go of my hands and retreats to the bed. He sits down, watching me with his intense blue eyes. I have to force myself not to shiver under his gaze.

*Focus on the wood, Rayne. Less thinking, more carving.*

"There!" I say about ten minutes later. "How does that look?" I hold the stake up for his perusal.

He walks over and takes it from me, examining it with a critical eye. "That's actually pretty good," he says, sounding a little too surprised for my liking. But secretly I'm pleased. "You're a natural."

"Natural Born Killahh!" I quip.

He chuckles. "Let's not get carried away. Just because you can carve a stake, doesn't mean you can stab someone with it."

"Gonna teach me that, too?" I tease.

His face darkens. "No."

The simple word seems to hold a whole lifetime of stories. He's definitely got to have some deep, dark torment and I'm dying to ask him what it is. But we barely know each other and also there's that whole thing about how we don't even like one another to contend with, so I decide to let him off the hook.

"Okay, no biggie," I say with a shrug. "Thanks for helping me carve it though."

"Not a problem," he says. "As long as you promise never to use it on me."

I'm about to crack a joke, but he looks too serious at the moment, so I let it go. "It's a deal," I say instead.

He smiles. "How about we go into the Post-Bite Lounge for a bit," he suggests. "See if we can pick up any gossip."

"Post-Bite Lounge?"

"Yes. You know how after giving blood at the Red Cross you can feel a little light-headed and queasy? Same thing after being sucked. So they have a lounge where they serve cookies and orange juice to the humans before they send them back into the world."

"Ah." Wow, these vamps think of everything, don't they? "Okay, cool. Let's lounge it."

I stand up and head toward the door.

"Uh, Rayne?"

I stop and turn around. "Yeah?"

He pauses, then says, "This is going to sound weird, but . . ."

"Everything is weird at this point. I doubt anything you could say could make it any weirder."

I can see Jareth's hard swallow from across the room. "You don't have a bite mark."

Okay. I was wrong. That is definitely weirder.

I cock my head in confusion. "What?"

"You're undercover as a human who likes being bitten by

vampires. You just spent time with a biter. Now we're going into the Post-Bite Lounge. People might notice that you don't have any marks on your neck."

"Oh." I reach up and touch my neck. Hm. He's right. "You think that'll raise a red flag?"

"I don't want to take any chances. We can't blow our cover. This is too important."

"Right. No. We shouldn't." I chew at my lower lip. "But . . . oh." I suddenly realize what he's suggesting. Am I up for that? To be bitten by him? I guess I don't have a choice, do I? Sacrifices for the cause and all that.

"Come here," Jareth instructs.

I walk over to the bed and sit down beside him. "Is this gonna hurt?" I ask, realizing I'm trembling. What is wrong with me? I've wanted to be bitten by a vampire for like EVER. Now I'm finally getting my chance. Of course, this type of bite won't turn me into a vampire. You have to be injected with their blood for that. But still . . . how cool, right?

So why am I *sooo* nervous?

"My fangs have an instant numbing solution that's injected at the moment of penetration. You won't feel a thing."

"Oh. Okay," I say, not feeling all that much better for some reason.

Jareth reaches over and brushes my hair away from my neck. I suddenly feel open. Exposed. Vulnerable. I swallow hard and close my eyes. I can feel his breath on my neck as he lowers his head. His lips brush lightly against my sensitive skin and I involuntarily let out a shiver.

"Ready?" he whispers softly. I can feel his lips forming the word against my flesh. It's kind of erotic, to tell you the truth. I bite down on my lower lip.

"Uh huh," I say, my voice suddenly as squeaky as Sunny's.

Moments later I feel a little pressure on my neck. Just a pinch and then . . . ecstasy.

I am so not going to be able to describe to you guys how awesome it feels to be bitten by a vampire. There aren't human words. It's better than Oreo ice cream sliding down your throat on a hot summer's day. Better than slipping into a steamy bathtub on a crisp fall afternoon. Better than curling up by a fire on a freezing winter's night.

It's better than anything I can possibly think of. Not that at that moment there's much thinking going on in my head. I'm just enjoying. Completely and utterly enjoying the sensations coursing through my veins.

It's heaven. Absolute heaven.

My head lolls backward and I let out a moan of pleasure. "Oh, god," I cry. "Don't stop."

But he does. I guess he has to, seeing as he's not out to drain me dry. Not that I'd have minded being drained dry at that particular moment. In fact, I would have embraced my death with open arms if that sensation were to continue. Now

I totally understand why it was easy for vampires to survive in the old days when they didn't have blood donors.

Once bitten, totally smitten.

His fangs retract. The electric current zapping through me clicks off like a light switch. The pleasure is gone. The ecstasy evaporates. I feel empty and alone and needy and desperate for more. No wonder this place is so popular. One bite and I already feel completely addicted.

I lift my head and open my eyes, looking over at Jareth. He's wiping his mouth, looking horrified and flushed and flustered beyond belief.

"Uh, there you go. You're bitten," he mumbles. He draws in a deep breath and pulls out a handkerchief, dabbing his sweaty forehead. Evidently the experience did something to him as well. Which makes me feel better, in a way. I'd hate to have succumbed to that rapture, only to find him all nonchalant and superior afterward.

I reach up to feel my neck, pressing my fingers against the tiny bite holes. "That was incredible," I murmur. "Amazing. I've never felt anything like it. Does it always feel that good? Or just the first time?"

"I certainly don't know," Jareth says in a totally unwarranted grumpy voice. He rises from the bed and walks toward the door. "I was only bitten once. When I was turned."

"Oh, right. Of course. Well, let me tell you, that totally rocked my world. You're good at the biteage, dude."

"I beg of you. Don't ever, ever call me dude again."

I sigh. "Sorry. But I was trying to give you a compliment."

"None necessary. It's just business. Nothing more."

"I know, but . . ." Why do I suddenly feel kind of hurt? He's right. This was obviously just for the job. To look legit. Nothing more. But still, it felt so intimate. . . .

I shake my head. *Earth to Rayne. Come in, Rayne.* We don't even like this dude—er, guy. So there is absolutely no reason to be upset. Just get the job done. Impress the council and you'll be assigned a real blood mate. Someone compatible to you DNA-wise. And then you can bite each other 'til the bats come home.

"Okay, fine. Let's go to the lounge."

I follow him out the door and down the corridor until we get to a room labeled LOUNGE. I've got to admit, I'm looking forward to the cookies and orange juice snack at this point. The bite, with all its euphoria, definitely left me feeling weak in the knees. I wonder how much blood he took from me. I wonder if he thought I tasted good. If they even care about that.

I wonder if he wishes he could bite me again.

Not that I care. Really.

The lounge is decked out like the rest of the Blood Bar, in red and black, but it's more relaxing looking than the formal sitting room lobby. There's a lot of smooshy velvet couches and little end tables with tea candles are scattered around the room. The candlelight is all the illumination the place has got and so all the inhabitants look a bit haunted and hollow-eyed. Or maybe that's just due to the fact they've been half drained dry a few minutes earlier.

I make a beeline for an empty couch across the room. I plop down, pulling my feet up and under me. Jareth heads to the bar on the far side of the room and returns a moment later with some juice and Ritz crackers.

"No Oreos, huh?" I ask as I take the plate from him and start chowing on the crackers. I slurp down some juice.

"Could you at least try to chew with your mouth closed?" Jareth hisses, taking a seat beside me. I roll my eyes. God, how can someone so sexy be so uptight and annoying? I mean, it's not like we're on a date, right? My actions should not have any reflection on him. And even if they do, who cares? We're at a freaking bite bar in the worst section of town. I say, in this sitch, it's safe to leave Miss Manners at the door.

Choosing to ignore him, I instead glance around the room, hoping to pick up some revealing scraps of conversation that might clue us into Maverick's evil plan. But it seems luck is not being a lady tonight. No one's saying a word.

"Wait a second," Jareth says, his eyes falling on two girls across the room. They're both gothed out and channeling Nicole Richie and Lindsay Lohan in their scrawniness, but they're definitely human.

"What?"

"I recognize those two. They're donors for my friend Kristoff."

"Yeah?" I ask, peering at the girls. "But that doesn't make sense."

FYI: A donor is a human who voluntarily signs up to be a regular blood source for a vampire. Each vamp has his own stable of donors. This way they don't bite unwilling people, like you see in the movies. It's all very civilized and there are blood tests and contracts and the donors make pretty good dough for their services.

But why would two donors be at the Blood Bar? They already get sucked by their vamp on a regular basis. There's no way they have that much blood to spare.

"That's a huge contract violation," Jareth says, peering at the girls. "What if they came down with some disease? They could infect Kristoff."

"Do you want to say anything to them?"

"No. It's not my place. And it would blow our cover. But I will certainly be reporting the incident tomorrow to Kristoff. He will have to let them go."

I stare at the two girls. They don't look all that well—even for Donor Chicks, who always look slightly anemic. Even under the dim lighting I can see the dark rings around their eyes and a slightly green tone to their skin.

Curiouser and curiouser, as Alice in Wonderland would say. . . .

\* \* \*

Anyway, that's all to report for now. More tomorrow, I'm sure. At least Jareth and I seem to have reached some kind of truce. We're never going to be BFFs, but at least we're not at each other's throats. Well, maybe that's a bad analogy . . . I mean, let's be honest here. Annoying or not, I'd let him be at my throat any day of the week. ;-)

**POSTED BY RAYNE McDONALD @ 1 A.M.**
**ONE COMMENT:**

**AstrydGrrl777 says . . .**
You got bit by a vampire! How cool is that? I'm sooooo jealous! What did it feel like? I mean, I know you kinda described it, but we want details! Lots of intimate, personal, embarrassing details! Come on, girl! Spill!!

# 11

## I Can't Breathe!

OMG! So I'm like almost asleep and I hear a car pull up. Mom! I jump out of bed and run to my window, hoping to get a good look at the date.

The front spotlight flickers on, illuminating two figures on the front porch. Two figures kissing, to be precise.

At first I'm overjoyed that my mom has found a boyfriend and is at last getting her groove on. But then I look closer. As the boyfriend in question pulls away, I get a good glimpse of his face for the first time. A face I'd recognize anywhere.

And suddenly I can't breathe.

I've got to IM Sunny. Now!

**POSTED BY RAYNE McDONALD @ 1:33 A.M.**
**TWO COMMENTS:**

**ButterfliQT says . . .**
ARGH! What is it? You can't leave us hanging like that! Who is it? It's not your Trig teacher, is it? The one you and Spider were talking about sleeping with? That'd be sooo nasty! Please post more and tell us it's not your Trig teacher!

**Rayne says . . .**
Don't worry—it's not my Trig teacher. And just FYI, I don't know about Spider, but I'd rather take an F than come within ten feet of Mr. McFee. I don't do balding mullets.

# 12

## Do Boyfriends Bite?

No time to explain. Pasting in chat transcript with Sunny to fill you in. This is huge. HUGE! And really, really, really BAD!

**RAYNIEDAY:** Sunny, are you awake?

**RAYNIEDAY:** Sunny, if you're not awake, wake up now! It's important.

**RAYNIEDAY:** SUNNY!!!!

**SUNSHINEBABY:** What the heck are you IM'ing me for at 2am?

**RAYNIEDAY:** I need to talk to you. It's an emergency.

**SUNSHINEBABY:** Uh, okay. But why not just walk across

the hall and knock on my door? It's not like I'm in Topeka.

**RAYNIEDAY:** Cause Mom's home. She might hear me.

**SUNSHINEBABY:** She'll hear tiptoed steps, but not the loud, obnoxious IM beeps coming from our computers?

**RAYNIEDAY:** So turn your sound down. Jeesh. You and technology. And hurry up. This can't wait.

**SUNSHINEBABY:** Okay, okay. Hang on.

**RAYNIEDAY:** . . .

**SUNSHINEBABY:** Okay, done. Now what's so important?

**RAYNIEDAY:** I don't know how to tell you this, but . . .

**SUNSHINEBABY:** Oh, god, Rayne, just spit it out. It's 2am and I've got a field hockey game tomorrow.

**RAYNIEDAY:** Hmph. This is so much more important than a field hockey game. Mom's dating a vampire.

**SUNSHINEBABY:** Field hockey is too import— WHAT?!??!

**RAYNIEDAY:** I told you it was important. But no. You never believe me. . . .

**SUNSHINEBABY:** Wait. Focus. I don't understand? How can she be dating a vampire?

**RAYNIEDAY:** She just got home. I spied out my window at them kissing.

**SUNSHINEBABY:** You know, that's pretty rude, Rayne. Whether we like Mom dating or not, she deserves our respect and privacy.

**RAYNIEDAY:** Are you going to listen to me about our mom

dating the undead or just lecture on parental etiquette all night?

**SUNSHINEBABY:** Fine. Go on.

**RAYNIEDAY:** So the guy pulls away and I get a good glimpse of his face. And I recognize him immediately. I saw him my first night at the Blood Bar. He was sort of standing in a corner, surveying the place. I'm thinking he works there as, like, a manager or something.

**SUNSHINEBABY:** OMG! So he's not only a vampire, he's a bad vampire. One of Maverick's men.

**RAYNIEDAY:** Yeah. That's what I was thinking. He probably thinks by getting close to Mom he can get close to you and then get close to Magnus.

**SUNSHINEBABY:** Wow. What are we going to do? We can't just tell Mom she's dating Dracula.

**RAYNIEDAY:** No. But we have to do something.

**SUNSHINEBABY:** Maybe he's not a vampire. Maybe he's a human who likes to be bit by them. You know, a customer.

**RAYNIEDAY:** It's possible. But I don't know. And really, it doesn't seem that good either way, now does it?

**SUNSHINEBABY:** Wow. This is just like what happened on *The Lost Boys*.

**RAYNIEDAY:** *The Lost Boys?*

**SUNSHINEBABY:** Vampire movie from the eighties? With Kiefer Sutherland? Jeesh, Rayne, I thought you watched all those movies.

**RAYNIEDAY:** I try to stick to vampire classics. Bela Lugosi. Maybe some Christopher Lee. Jack Bauer from *24* just doesn't scream VAMP to me.

**SUNSHINEBABY:** Fine. But you should watch it. Like, tomorrow. It's totally the same thing. The kids' mom starts dating this guy and they think he's a vampire so they try to prove it.

**RAYNIEDAY:** How do they do that?

**SUNSHINEBABY:** Um, I can't remember exactly. Garlic. Holy water. Stuff like that, I think. Really good movie, even if they do all have big hair and bad clothes.

**RAYNIEDAY:** So you're suggesting we try that stuff on the date? Hm. Not a bad idea. Then we'd have proof. I mean, I'd like to have proof before I go and stake Mom's BF.

**SUNSHINEBABY:** Yes. Seems wise.

**RAYNIEDAY:** Sigh. Poor Mom. She was so excited about the guy. It's going to suck to have to slay him.

**SUNSHINEBABY:** But it's in her best interest. After all, he doesn't really like her. He's just using her to get to me.

**RAYNIEDAY:** Right. True. We have the best intentions.

**SUNSHINEBABY:** Anyway—I've got to get some sleep. School tomorrow. Goodnight, Rayne.

**RAYNIEDAY:** You're such a nerd. I can't believe you can think of school at a time like this.

**SUNSHINEBABY:** GOOD NIGHT, RAYNE.

**RAYNIEDAY:** Sigh. Night, Sun.

**SUNSHINEBABY HAS LEFT THE CHAT.**

**POSTED BY RAYNE McDONALD @ 2 A.M.**
**TWO COMMENTS:**

**Just Curious says . . .**
Wow, what's with you chicks? You're all hooking up with vamps? Is there something in the McDonald family water supply? Is your blood supersweet?

**Rayne says . . .**
First of all, we are NOT all hooking up with vampires. Me, for example, the one person in the family who WANTS to hook up with a vampire, has had absolutely no luck in getting one near me. All I get are idiots like Magnus, who go off and bite the wrong girl, or losers like Jareth, who have so many issues they can't see the delectable treat right in front of them. No, it appears it's only McDonald women who aren't interested in being with vamps that have any luck in hooking them. So very sad.

# 13

## Breakfast Bites

So I wake up this morning bright and early, throw on a black crocheted sweater and a short black skirt. I roll on my fishnet tights and lace up my combat boots. Then I head to my bathroom for my morning makeup routine. It takes a lot of time to become "me" in the A.M. But it's worth it.

Sunny, whose idea of morning preparation involves slipping on a T-shirt and jeans and running a comb through her hair, is already downstairs, dressed and picking at some godawful concoction my mom whipped up. Mom makes very interesting breakfasts with the food she buys at the co-op and we're her guinea pigs. When Sunny had been turning vampire, Mom experimented with this garlic breakfast scramble.

The smell alone sent Sunny scrambling to the bathroom to retch her guts out. She claims that was just because of her burgeoning aversion to garlic, but honestly it could have just been the recipe and Mom's attempt to cook.

"So what's the special of the morning?" I ask, sliding into my chair. I'm famished. Nothing she can possibly come up with will make me lose my appetite today.

"Well, it doesn't really have an official name," Mom says, dishing some of the unidentified mush from the frying pan onto a plate. "But the cook at the commune used to refer to it as hippie hash."

Then again, maybe I'll skip first period and hit Dunkin' Donuts on the way to school.

"So how'd your date go?" I ask, trying not to wrinkle my nose as she puts the foul smelling scramble in front of me.

She sets another plate in front of her own spot and sits down between Sunny and me. I glance over at my sister and notice that while the food is being moved around her plate, it's not going into her mouth.

"Great," Mom says, her eyes shining. "We went out to the nicest restaurant. Of course, it was a steak house. He's evidently a big steak eater. Says he loves them really rare."

I try to catch Sunny's eyes. See? Rare steak. The only thing vampires enjoy eating, as it's so bloody.

"He took you to a steak house?" I ask. Mom's a strict vegetarian, of course. Poor woman. "Didn't you tell him you don't eat meat? That you belong to PETA? That you think the chemicals found in cattle are mind-controlling hormones injected by the government to sedate the human race while big business goes around and trashes our world?"

"It's okay," Mom says, of course completely excusing her date's major faux pas. "I just had a potato and vegetables. It was very good."

Wow. Mom must really have a thing for this guy. She would never go to a slaughter house with just anyone. It's going to be sad to disappoint her. Not that she'll be disappointed when she finds out he's a thousand years old and undead. Oh, well.

"Then what did you do?"

"He took me out to this elegant club where they had an old-fashioned band and dancing. He waltzes like a dream."

Hm. Probably 'cause he was around when they invented the dance and has had a thousand years of practice.

"But you hate waltzing. And classical music. In fact, isn't your saying, 'If it's not Jefferson Airplane, it's crap'?"

She narrows her eyes. "Rayne, I'm an adult with a wide variety of interests. I had a good time. Don't spoil it because you feel uncomfortable I went on a date."

Sigh. Here she goes. Her voice sounds all tight. I knew she'd jump to that conclusion.

"I'm fine with you having a date. I just want to make sure

he's treating you right." And doesn't spend his days sleeping in a coffin. . . .

"Well, you don't have to worry. He's the perfect gentleman. You'll see, tonight."

"Tonight?" Sunny's eyes and my eyes meet across the table. I'm sure mine are as wide as hers.

Mom laughs. "Yes, tonight. I invited him over for dinner. I promised I could cook him a tofu steak that's just as delicious as one made from the slaughter of innocent animals."

Wow. I bet the vamp is really looking forward to that! But tonight! That doesn't give Sunny and me any time to plan. Unless . . .

I break out into a coughing fit.

"Oh, man," I say between chokes. "I've had this horrible cough. Just horrible. And I don't feel very well either."

"But you were just—?" Sunny starts in. I kick her under the table. Hard. Her eyes light up. And her coughs start coming.

My mom looks from one hacking daughter to the other. "Are you two okay?" she asks. "It's not the hash, is it?"

It probably would be the hash if either of us had actually shoveled any of it into our mouths, which in hindsight may have made the sickness a tad more authentic, but too late now.

"No. It's just, I think I'm coming down with something."

"Maybe you should stay home from school," Mom says, looking worried. "Neither of you sound too good."

"No, I want to go to school," I say, pausing to slump in my chair and close my eyes. "I really hate missing school."

"If you're sick, you need to stay home," Mom commands, reaching over to feel my forehead with the back of her hand. "You feel warm, Rayne." It's amazing what the power of suggestion can do to a parent. "You, too, Sunny," she says, switching to my twin.

"But I love school, Mom," Sunny whines. Gah! Overkill, much? I kick her under the table again. For someone starring in the school play, she's not much of an actress.

"Mom's right, Sun," I interject, to stop her performance. "If we go to school, it might get worse. We could be contagious even. One day of rest now can save us from a weeklong absence down the road."

Mom takes a bite of her hash and nods. "Unfortunately, I can't stay home to take care of you guys," she says, as if that would be something either of us would want. "I've got to get to work."

"It's okay, Mom," I say, patting her on the arm. "We'll probably be sleeping most of the day anyway."

"I hope so." She rises from her seat, kisses both of us on the tops of our heads, and brings her mostly untouched plate over to the sink. Evidently this time even she didn't like her recipe, not that she'd ever admit that to us. "There's OJ in the fridge and some veggie burgers in the freezer if you get hungry later."

"Thanks, Mom."

"Do you think I should cancel having my friend come over?" she asks, scraping her leftovers into the compost bin. "I mean, if you two are sick . . ."

"No, no," Sunny says, before I can kick her a third time. "We'll feel better by then, I'm sure."

Great. Way to buy us more time, Sun.

"Okay. Well, you let me know," Mom says, sounding relieved. "Call me at work if you take a turn for the worse and would rather just lay low."

So she goes to work and now Sunny and I are home alone. Sunny rinses our breakfast plates and I run up to my room for my secret stash of strawberry Pop-Tarts. After toasting, we rendezvous in the living room, me on the couch, Sunny on the lounger.

"So what are we going to do?" my sister asks, mouth full of Pop-Tart. "He's coming over tonight. That doesn't give us much time."

"Right." I break my pastry in half, licking the strawberry filling. "What about calling Magnus? Certainly he could recognize a fellow vamp."

"Yeah, but it's daytime. He won't be up and about 'til well after dinner."

"Oh, yeah. Duh." I smack myself on the forehead. That was stupid.

"What about you?" Sunny asks. "Aren't you the knower of all things vamp? The proud graduate of Vampire School? Won't you be able to tell on sight whether the guy sleeps in a coffin or not?"

I shrug. "Not necessarily. A vampire can cast what's called a 'glamour' on themselves to make them look human if they need to. That's how they can walk among us and no one's the wiser. And I doubt the guy's going to show up to dinner sporting his fangs."

"Great." Sunny sighs. "What are we going to do then?"

"What about that movie you were talking about again? *The Lost Boys?*"

"Yeah. We could rent that. . . ."

"No time. Netflix takes at least a day to deliver."

Sunny laughs. "You ever hear of a video store, Rayne?"

D'oh. "Oh. Right. Forgot about those." Stores that you can go into and rent DVDs instead of having them mailed to your door. How cute and retro. "Do they still exist?"

"I think there's a Blockbuster downtown."

"Okay, cool." I pull my feet out from under me. "So you go run to the Blockbuster and rent every vampire movie you can find. I'll go on the Internet and research what I can from here."

"It's a plan."

It wasn't exactly a plan, but it was a start. Operation Date with Dracula was on.

**POSTED BY RAYNE McDONALD @ 12 P.M.**
**THREE COMMENTS:**

**CTU-in-TrainingGrrl says . . .**
Wait—you mean Jack Bauer was in movies before he became a CTU agent? Vampire movies? Whoa. I've got to update my Netflix queue ASAP!!

**StarrMoonUnit says . . .**
Can you post the recipe for hippie hash? That sounds de-lish! I mean, I've had hippie brownies before and mmmmm. . . .

**Rayne says . . .**
Hey, CTU girl, you are aware that *24* is just a TV show, right? I mean, it's not even a reality one. It's got, like, a script. Jack Bauer is some dude named Kiefer Sutherland and evidently he's been in a billion movies and even dated Julia Roberts back in the day. Sorry to disappoint.

　　And P.S., StarrMoonUnit? Hate to disappoint you as well, but there's actually no hash in the hippie hash. . . .

# 14

## The Not-So-Lost Girls

The doorbell rings at six o'clock and Sunny and I are ready. In fact, if Dracula himself were to bust through the door, I think we'd actually have a chance of defeating the guy.

First up, we're both wearing necklaces made out of garlic under our hoodies. We've got holy water (which we snuck in and "borrowed" from St. Patrick's Church down the road) locked and loaded into our Super Soaker Triple Shot water guns. I'm wearing rosary beads and Sunny's got on her cross necklace. In short, together we're every vampire's worst nightmare.

"Can you get the door?" Mom asks from the kitchen. While we've been preparing, she's been running around trying to get the meal together. I felt bad not helping her, but we had too much to do on our end. I did agree to stir the vegan marinade (not sure why tofu needs to be marinated, but whatever) while Mom went upstairs to change. That gave me a chance to add a few cloves of garlic to the mix.

"Girls?"

"I'll get it, Mom." Sunny jumps up, ready to oblige with the door opening.

"Wait!" I cry. "Didn't *The Lost Boys* teach you anything?" According to the movie, the boys' plan to determine whether their mom's BF was a vamp was foiled because they invited him into the house. Evidently if you let a vampire in, you're powerless against him. "We must learn from the lessons the bad eighties movies teach us."

"Uh, right," Sunny says, sitting back down. The doorbell rings again. She picks up the DVD case and skims the back. "Though did you really think it was that bad? I thought it held up kind of well, considering it was made, like, twenty years ago."

"Sunny! Rayne! Answer the door!" Hm. Mom's not sounding as sweet and patient anymore.

Sunny sets down the case. "Anyway, what if Mom lets him in? Does that mean the house is still safe for him? That anything we do won't work?"

I scratch my head. "I don't know. The movie never addressed that possibility. Maybe we should go to the door and refuse him entrance. Just to make sure. Then if Mom lets him in, she'll be the only one rendered powerless."

"Good idea."

We jump up from our seats and rush to the door. We stare at it for a moment, then at each other, both wondering what we would find on the other side. Would he be elegant and poised? Would he try to hypnotize us with mesmerizing eyes? What if he had one of the hounds of hell with him, like the boyfriend in the movie, ready to attack? Or maybe he'd be full-on vamped already, having decided to skip dinner and go right for our necks . . . as dessert.

You never knew with an evil vampire, now did you?

"Okay, let's do this," I say. I take a deep breath, then wrap my fingers around the handle and pull it open, revealing the man on the other side of the door.

Sunny looks at the guy, then at me, one eyebrow raised in doubt. I know what she's thinking. The guy doesn't exactly look like a creature of the night. Out of his tux, he looks more like . . . well, an accountant. Maybe it was the lighting in the Blood Bar that made him look so commanding. Or the tux. Dressed in a pair of beige slacks and a button-down shirt, I gotta admit, he just doesn't give off the same ghoulie glow.

Or maybe it's the pocket protector that's throwing us off.

He's also . . . tanned looking. But, of course, that could totally be faked with Jergens. There's this girl at school, Denise, who always looks like she's been vacationing in the

Bahamas, but it's totally bogus. The girl has never been south of Jersey.

In short, the guy looks nothing like a blood sucker. But that could be his clever disguise. One thing I've learned in the vamp world—no one is as they seem. The former Master of the Blood Coven, Lucifent, looked like the little boy from *The Sixth Sense*. The former slayer, Bertha, resembled a hippo more than Sarah Michelle Gellar. And, of course, Jareth, who is uber-hot and channeling Jude Law, is in actuality the most annoying, uptight, jerky vampire in the known universe.

Not that I've been thinking of Jareth. In fact, I'd nearly forgotten he even exists up until this moment. I'm not even disappointed that he had a council meeting tonight and couldn't meet me at the Blood Bar. In fact, I'm relieved. Very relieved not to have to see him again. . . .

Sorry, tangent. Back to what happened.

"Hi. I'm David," Mr. Accountant Nerd says, incidentally (or not so incidentally) giving the same name as Kiefer's character in *The Lost Boys*. He's carrying a bouquet of dark red roses. The color of blood, I might add. "You must be Sunshine and Rayne?"

Hm. He knows our names. Very interesting. Then again, I guess Mom could have told him. . . .

"I'm Sunny. She's Rayne," Sunny says, helpfully. I wonder for a moment whether she's been hypnotized to do his bidding and tell him all, then I decide it's just typical Sunny, being overly friendly.

David looks from me to Sunny and back again. "Um, would you like to invite me in?" he asks, looking a little doubtful.

Ah-ha! I shoot Sunny a triumphant glance. He used the exact words! He asked to be invited in! I knew it! I knew he was a vampire.

"It's pretty wet out here," David adds.

Whoops. I'd been so wrapped up in what he looked like I hadn't even noticed the torrential downpour the guy is standing in. Guess at least we could rule out him being a witch. He so would have melted by now.

Still, that doesn't mean the plan has changed any.

"Actually, no. We can't invite you in," I say, trying to sound as apologetic, but firm as possible. "We are not inviting you in."

"Right," Sunny adds. "In fact, we personally, Rayne and I, are denying you entrance to our house. If someone else wants to let you in—like Mom or something—well, we can't stop her. But that doesn't mean we're inviting you in. It's her decision. Which is separate from ours."

"Right. What she said," I agree. "We cannot invite you in to our house. Nothing personal. We just . . . won't. Can't."

"What's going on out here?" Mom comes up from behind us. She surveys the scene. Us blocking the door like two identical sentries. David standing outside in the rain with his wilted roses. "Girls? Why are you standing in front of the door?"

Caught. We jump aside, both with matching guilty expressions.

"The girls were just saying that it was up to the lady of the house to invite me in," says Mr. Smooth, tossing us a little wink.

Mom looks over at us, her eyes narrowed. She's wondering what we're up to, I'm sure, and doesn't look the least bit amused.

"O-kay," she says at last. "Well, please come in, David. Before you get soaked to the bone."

Bingo. She says the magic words and the vampire steps over the threshold and into our house.

Ugh—hang on. Getting IM'ed. I'll write more in a few. . . .

**POSTED BY RAYNE McDONALD @ 10 P.M.**
**ONE COMMENT:**

**ThisVampsGotBack says . . .**
You know, you can be very discriminatory when it comes to your narrow definition of an appropriate-looking vampire. First poor Francis, who has a little extra muscle, and now this

David guy, who because he wears glasses is all of a sudden Clark Kent. Vampires are not all Goths. They come in every shape and size and race. I'd appreciate a little more tact when you describe our kind from now on.

# 15

## Dinner with Dracula

Okay, sorry, I'm back. Ready to recap dinner with Dracula.

So we all go into the dining room, which for a moment I don't even recognize. We're not all that formal in the McDonald house, you see, and we usually sit at the kitchen table. The dining room is reserved for big projects like 1,000-piece puzzles or papier-mâché recreations of Custer's Last Stand or whatever school project we're currently working on. It's usually messy and informal and covered in books and jackets and other bric-a-brac.

Mom's totally cleaned house. I actually think I see things sparkling.

I don't know how she managed to work all day and still

have time to cook and tidy up. I feel a stab of guilt that we didn't help her, but what could we do? We had major preps to take care of. She'll thank us someday. When we save her from becoming a snack. When she gets to live to see us help clean the house another day.

"Everyone take a seat and dinner will be right up," Mom says, motioning to the table. Wow. Fancy water goblets and matching plates. Who knew we had matching plates? I wonder if she borrowed from the neighbor. And candles! In the center of the table sits a beautiful lilac and candle centerpiece. Did she actually make that? Candles and flowers and matching plates—oh, my! This guy is morphing Mom into Martha Stewart. Too bad he's an evil dark lord of the night or I'd be welcoming his influence with open arms.

Sunny and I watch as David picks his seat. Then we choose seats right across from him, so we can check out his every move. If he even dares to sneeze, we're going to catalog it for future study.

Mom sniffs the air, a puzzled look falling across her face. "What's that smell?" she asks. "Do you guys smell something?"

Ah-ha! I elbow Sunny in the ribs. "Bad breath," I whisper. "That was a sign of someone being a vampire in *The Lost Boys*."

"Puh-leeze. That's just a movie thing," Sunny hisses back. "Magnus doesn't have bad breath."

Maybe not. I've never gotten close enough to smell it. But still, I'm not entirely convinced. And after all, Mom did say she smelled something and it certainly isn't Sunny and me.

"It smells like a garlic farm in here," Mom adds.

Okay. Maybe it is Sunny and me.

"Uh, we ordered in some pizza for lunch," Sunny says. "Extra, extra, extra garlic."

David wrinkles his nose. "Ugh. Sounds terrible," he says with a small laugh. Sunny and I exchange glances.

"I agree," Mom says, giggling like a school girl. I have to resist the urge to roll my eyes. She's got it bad for this guy.

"Actually, I have a garlic allergy," David says, further damning himself to the dark side. "That's one of the reasons I shop at the co-op. I can get foods that don't contain certain ingredients that would cause me to have an allergic reaction."

I exchange an excited glance at Sunny. A garlic allergy? A little bit of a convenient excuse, don't you think? Good way to pass off to gullible humans that you're not a doomed creature of the darkness set to eat our mom.

We're wise to you, Vamp Nerd.

"Well, you won't find any garlic in tonight's dinner," Mom says, having no clue about my secret last-minute add to the marinade. "Or any preservatives. I don't trust ingredients I can't pronounce."

"I agree. In fact, this may sound crazy, but I've always believed that the food industry could be being paid off by the pharmaceutical companies to make people get illnesses like cancer or high blood pressure. The more sick people, the more medication sales." He chuckles, looking down at his plate. "Probably a little out there, I know."

Oh, no. Ohhh, no. Mom's eyes are lighting up like a Christmas tree. Here we go.

"I've always said the exact same thing!" she cries. She turns to us. "Haven't I, girls? In fact, just the other day when Raynie was coloring her hair with some drugstore dye . . ."

I tune her out. I've heard her conspiracy theories one too many times. I can't believe David here thinks the same thing. I didn't know anyone could be as flaky as Mom. Too bad he's an evil blood-sucking beast, 'cause they'd be a great fit.

The oven timer dings just as they're getting to the part where the government is working with alien nations to secretly control the economy of the universe. Mom heads into the kitchen.

"So," David turns to us, all ready to be Mr. Friendly. "What do you girls enjoy doing for fun?"

I'm about to say, "I slay vampires," but Sunny beats me to the punch with a much wiser answer. She grabs the cross on her rosary beads and holds it up to David.

"Mostly we pray to God," she says, smiling sweetly. "Don't you just love my rosary beads?"

David doesn't break out into a full sweat or anything, but he suddenly looks mighty nervous.

"Have you given your life to the Lord Jesus?" I ask, taking

my cue and grabbing my own cross. "He died to save your soul, you know." Not that you have one, Vamp Nerd.

David swallows hard. You can totally tell he wants to run screaming from the room. His insides are probably boiling, just from the proximity of the crosses.

He is so definitely a vampire.

I'm just about to ask him if he'd like to say a few Hail Marys with me, but then Mom returns. Which is convenient, in a way, since I actually have no idea how to say a Hail Mary. We borrowed the rosary beads from Old Sister Anne, the retired nun down the street who's been using them to pray for our family's soul for years.

"What are you girls wearing?" Mom asks, looking more than a tad confused.

Caught. Sunny turns beet red and I'm sure I'm the same. "Uh, rosary beads?" I say. "You know, for when we . . . confess?" Is that what you do with rosary beads? We were brought up in an ultra-liberal church where most of the choir members are drag queens and are thus ultra-clueless to the tenets of the Catholic church.

Mom raises a questioning eyebrow, then turns to David. "Kids," she says, shaking her head. "We're actually lapsed Unitarians. We don't use rosary beads."

David smiles indulgently at her. "I'm sorry to say I'm a bit of an agnostic, myself," he says. "You'll never find me setting foot in a church."

Of course you wouldn't, Vamp Nerd. You'd probably spontaneously combust from the pure evilness that is in your soul.

"Well, in some respects, I believe religion has been set in place to sedate the unhappy masses so the government can control our lives," Mom theorizes as she dishes out the tofu steaks and vegan mashed potatoes.

"I completely agree with you," David says.

Oh, god. Here we go again.

Mom sits and the conversation goes back to the bizarre. For a vampire, David has a lot of out-there political opinions. Either that, or he's just trying to impress Mom. Which means he's done his research. Suddenly, this situation becomes a whole lot scarier. I wonder what he knows about me. About Sunny.

I do notice that the guy doesn't eat much dinner. He mostly pushes the food around on his plate. At first I think this could be another sign of vampirism, 'til I notice Sunny doing the same thing and realize it could just be Mom's cooking. I'm not too thrilled with it myself. Plus, he does take a confirmed bite or two.

The two grown-ups are so engrossed in their conversation that they don't notice as Sunny and I slip out of our seats. Mom's too wrapped up in Mr. Conspiracy Theory. In fact, she's almost glowing. I haven't seen her this happy in years. Really blows that I'm going to have to kill the guy.

Oh, well. It's for the best. But first we have to confirm our suspicions. I need to make sure the guy is one hundred percent evil vamp before I go whip out my stake.

We grab the Super Soakers we'd hid behind the couch. Time for Phase Two.

"Lock and load," I say, raising my gun.

She grins. "I'm so going to soak you!" she cries in an extra loud voice.

"Not if I soak you first!"

For the record, this was Sunny's plan. I personally didn't think anyone would buy that two sixteen-year-old girls would run around the house playing with water guns. Except, I guess, crazy Aunt Edna, who bought them for us. But she also bought us sweater sets in girls' size 6X, so I'm not sure she's aware that we've graduated from kindergarten yet.

The main floor of our house is all connected, each room leading into the next. So we split up. Sunny goes through the living room and I go through the kitchen, all the while yelling threats back and forth.

"Girls? What are you doing—?"

But suddenly Mom knows exactly what we're doing, though, of course, not what noble reason we have for doing it. We're in the dining room, one on each side of Vamp Nerd, spraying each other with water and "inadvertently" spraying him in the process.

He starts screaming like a little girl, putting his hands over his head. Sunny and I stop squirting.

"Argh! I'm soaked!" he cries.

Mom stares at him, then at us. I've never seen her look so upset. She looks like she doesn't know whether to cry or scream. "David! Are you okay?" she asks before turning to us. "Girls! What is going on here?" she demands. "What the hell do you think you're doing?"

"Uh, sorry, Mom. We were just playing around." 'Cause, um, sixteen-year-old girls always play with water guns at the dinner table. She's so not going to buy this.

David rises from his seat, shaking the water off. We stare at him, waiting to see what will happen. Will his skin start burning off his body 'cause of the holy water? Will he burst into flames?

I watch as red blotches start appearing on the guy's neck, spreading upward to his face. I knew it! The water burned him. He really is a vampire. I resist the urge to give Sunny a high five. The two of us rock. Mom is saved. She will so be thanking us later for this.

"Oh, David, I'm so sorry," Mom says. She grabs a handful of napkins and runs around the table to dab at his soaked clothes. I wonder if it wasn't overkill. Those Super Soakers really put out a good deal of $H_2O$. "I don't know what's gotten into them." She shoots Sunny and me death glares. "How about an apology, girls?"

"Actually, I'm not feeling very well," David says to my mom. "I, uh, think I should go."

"What's wrong with your face, David?" Sunny demands, not sounding all that apologetic. "Did the water burn?"

David reaches up to touch his face. His eyes widen. "I think I may be breaking out in hives!" he cries.

"Well, holy water can do that," I say, having no idea if that's true or not.

He ignores me. "Was there garlic in that tofu?"

Uh-oh.

"No. Definitely not!" Mom says, looking like she's going to cry. "David, you're really red. Maybe we should get you to a hospital."

"I can drive myself," he says grimly.

"I really don't—" Mom sighs. She gets the hint. "Okay. If you're sure . . ."

The speed by which David heads for the door makes it clear that he's pretty sure. He wants out of here. Not that I blame him. First garlic, then crosses, followed by holy water. He knows the stake can't be far behind. *Adios, vampiro.*

"Good-bye. I'll, uh, call you." He doesn't sound all that sincere.

"Bye, David. I really am sorry."

But David has already left the building.

We win.

Mom sinks into her seat and puts her head in her hands. We wait for her to yell. To scream. But she doesn't. She just starts to cry.

Oh, great.

"Sorry, Mom." What else can I say? I can't explain why we did what we did. Or that it's for her own good.

She looks up at me, her eyes red and her face blotchy. "Why, girls?" she asks. "Why would you do that?" She grabs a napkin and blows her nose. "You could have just told me you were uncomfortable with me dating. You didn't have to terrorize the guy. I really like him, you know?"

Ugh. I breathe out a frustrated breath. Now what? We've just scared off Mom's date, which is a good thing, seeing as he's pretty much confirmed as an evil vampire. But now she's hurt and upset and feels like we've betrayed her.

"He wasn't right for you," I say, putting an arm around her shoulders to try to comfort her. "You'll find someone else."

She looks up. "Wasn't right for me? He's perfect for me!"

Sigh. Just sigh. I open my mouth to try again, but nothing comes out. Sunny is edging out of the room, abandoning me to the tears. Coward!

"Look, girls. I'm not trying to replace your dad," she says. "I just . . . well, I get lonely sometimes. You have your own lives and are always out and I sit in the house by myself half the time. I'm not that old," she adds. "I'd like another chance at love. And I'm asking you guys to be okay with that."

Mom heads upstairs, slamming her bedroom door behind her. I sink into a dining room chair. Did we do the right thing? This is so hard. So, so hard. 'Cause I am okay with that. More than okay. In fact, I want nothing more than for my mom to meet a nice guy and live happily ever after. I just have one requirement. Prince Charming shouldn't be an evil vampire. Is that so much to ask?

Sunny reappears, her face white and her expression uber-serious. She's holding a beige jacket in her arms. David's jacket.

"He left his jacket?" I ask, raising an eyebrow. This could be interesting. "Did you search it?"

She nods slowly. "And I found something in his pocket," she says, handing a folded piece of paper to me. "Look at this."

I take it and unwrap it slowly, my eyes widening as I read. "Oh, my god," I whisper, looking up at Sunny, then back down at the paper.

"Yeah," she says solemnly.

The scrawled writing on the paper looks like a cheat sheet—like something a cheating student would bring to a test. And it's got information. Lots of personal information. About my mom. About Sunny. About me.

And about Magnus.

This is so not good.

**POSTED BY RAYNE McDONALD @ 10:30 P.M.**
**TWO COMMENTS:**

**CandyGrrl says . . .**
Ooh, that's sooo scary, Rayne! Do you think Maverick knows you're out to get him and sent a spy of his own? Good thing you scared the guy away! But what if he comes back?

**Angelbaby3234566 says . . .**
You know, now that I think about it, I think MY mom's new BF might be an evil vampire, too. I'm so renting *The Lost Boys* and trying your guys' techniques. Heck, even if he turns out to be human, maybe I'll be able to scare him away anyway, which is good enough 4 me.

# 16

## Way More Than Six Feet Under

That night Sunny calls Magnus and tells him about the David incident. He reassures her that everything will be okay and he'll assign some vamps to guard our house and some others to try to track the guy down. Unfortunately, we only know his first name so it's not like we can look up his address in the white pages. Sigh. I so should have staked him when I had the chance.

The next day my cell phone beeps as I'm getting out of school, informing me I have a text message. I scroll through and find it's from Jareth, of all people. (No idea how he got my mobile number, maybe Mom's right when she says there's just no privacy anymore.) The message itself is short and sweet:

## MEET ME AT CLUB FANG @ 7PM

For those of you who don't know, Club Fang is this way cool Goth club in Nashua, New Hampshire, that's also a big vamp hangout. Well, by night, anyway. During the day I think it doubles as a Knights of Columbus hall. Heh. If only the "knights" knew the antics that went on once the sun dipped below the horizon. They'd totally freak.

It's also the place where Magnus first accidentally bit Sunny and turned her into a vampire, but that's not such a fond memory for me so we won't be rehashing that.

I arrive at Club Fang, park the car, and pay my five bucks to go inside. They've got the smoke machines going and much of the dance floor is obscured by fog. Black lights shine down from the ceilings, casting purplish shadows everywhere. At the far end, a tubby DJ spins goth and electronica tunes. At the moment he's playing the Sisters of Mercy song "Temple of Love," which is one of my favorites. Not seeing Jareth around, I decide I might as well dance for a bit while waiting.

I love dancing. Swaying my body to deep, seductive music. Letting myself become one with the beat. Losing myself in the orchestra of light. I close my eyes and weave my arms through the air, floating through the ambient waves of sound. It's heavenly. All my troubles, all my stress, just float away into the night.

In the old days, like when my mom was a kid, people

always danced with a partner. Which is okay, I guess. But then you're worried about the proper steps and the other person's lead and stepping on their toes. When you're dancing with yourself, you have none of these concerns. You can just let go.

The song changes and I open my eyes. Responsibility replaces rhythm. As much as I'd like to dance all night, I've got to find Jareth. I scan the café side of the club, adorned with little tables covered by black tablecloths and lit by candles. Several vampy-looking patrons are sipping what appears to be a deep crimson wine. But the color looks a bit too dark to be your average merlot, if you know what I'm saying. Many have brought their donors with them. Usually pale, thin Goth girls who think it's oh-so-cool to sell their blood to a thirsty vamp. Most of the donors are total vamp wannabes. Ones who failed the certification program to become vampires themselves.

Maybe I should become a donor. Then I'd get to experience that amazing biting experience every night. Then again, that just rings a little too close to prostitution to me. The vamp would just be using me for blood.

No, I can wait. 'Til I'm assigned a new blood mate. Someone completely compatible with me who I can spend the rest of eternity with. Someone whose bites will actually mean something. I want that. I deserve that.

Anyway, no sign of Jareth, so I turn to head back out onto

the dance floor. It's there I spot him. At the far end of the room, lit by a black light, his pale skin is almost glowing. He's dressed simply, wearing a white pirate shirt with puffy sleeves and black pants. But he looks like a god as he sways under the light. His eyes are closed, his face a mask of ecstasy and concentration. He's got perfect moves, perfect rhythm. It's almost as if he's part of the music. I know that sounds weird, but it's hard to describe. Suffice it to say he looks beautiful. Absolutely stunning.

The Jareth I know is uptight and annoying. A total ass.

This is not the Jareth I know.

This is the Jareth I want to know.

I weave my way through the other dancers 'til I reach him. His eyes are still closed, and I notice he's wearing eyeliner. De-lish. I love a guy in eyeliner.

Not wanting to disturb his dance-induced trance, I merely pick up the beat myself, closing my own eyes, floating my arms through the air. Finding the music and making love to it. Letting the dark, melodious sounds take me away. To the place Jareth has found. Hoping I can find him there, too.

An arm wraps around my waist and a body presses against mine. I consider opening my eyes, but the feeling is too nice. The heat, the touch, the matching of my movements with his own.

Is it Jareth? It has to be Jareth. And he feels so good. So right. Just as I imagined he would.

I feel myself being pulled deeper and deeper inside the music. A rich darkness consumes me, pulling me toward a strange white light. I take back every single thing I said about it being better to dance alone. It's better to dance with Jareth. One hundred million, billion, gazillion times better.

"You're a good dancer," his voice whispers in my ear.

"You, too," I whisper back, wanting this moment to last forever. Wow. This is so not the Jareth I know, that's for sure. Who knew he was so deeply and darkly romantic. So—

"Rayne, are you going to waste the entire night on the dance floor? Or can we get some work done here?"

My eyes flutter open at the unmistakable voice. I glance at my dance partner. Uh-oh.

It's not Jareth. Not even close. Ew! I've been grinding with some totally random vamp who's not even cute. Gr-*oss*. And uber-disappointing.

I push the guy away, annoyed. I look over to see Jareth staring disapprovingly at me, arms folded across his chest. He looks terribly annoyed.

"Jareth?" My head's still foggy from the dancing. "I thought—"

"If you've had your fun, I suggest we get down to business," he shouts over the music.

"Hey, buddy," says my accidental dance partner. "She's dancing with me."

Jareth rolls his eyes. "She can marry you, for all I care.

Have babies. Live happily ever after in a white-picketed sub-urban McMansion. But for right now, I have important business to discuss with her and she's coming with me."

He grabs me roughly by the arm and proceeds to drag me to the café side of the club.

"Get your hands off me," I protest, annoyed at his possessiveness. If I didn't know better, I'd say he was totally jealous. But that's stupid, right? I mean, we don't even know each other, really. Or like each other. We shared one bite. And it was performed under necessity, not attraction. Well, not total attraction, anyway. Okay, fine. I was attracted. But for him it was just part of our cover. At least I think so.

Still, for some weird reason he's making me feel totally guilty. As if I was, like, cheating on him or something. Which is so stupid. We're totally not going out. We're not even friends. We're just partners thrown together to solve a vampire mystery. After that's over, we'll part ways. Forever. And I do mean forever.

Jareth still looks pouty as he sits down in his seat. I decide to make peace. Even if he doesn't have any right to be pissed at me.

"I was watching you," I say. "You're an amazing dancer."

"Thanks," he says, still sounding a bit on the grumpy side. "It's something I enjoy."

I smile. "Me, too. I sometimes feel like dancing is the only way I can be at total peace with myself. It's like the world stops while you're dancing. And nothing matters but the music."

He pauses for a moment, then agrees. "I know what you mean. Sometimes I come here by myself. When the world is too much to deal with. I can escape for a few hours. Forget all the pain."

He stops talking and stares at his hands. I wonder, not for the first time, what secret hurt he's hiding and whether we'll ever be close enough for him to share it with me.

I decide to confess. Maybe my humiliation will cheer him a bit.

"You know, I had my eyes closed," I say. "Stupidly, I thought that guy who came up and started dancing with me was you."

Jareth looks up, raising a perfectly arched eyebrow. "Me?"

"Yeah." I'm hoping the bar's dim lighting is hiding my blush.

"Would you . . . have liked it to be me?"

Gah! He did not just go there. Now my face is burning. "Uh . . ."

"You're all red, my dear." His smile tells me he's enjoying teasing me, seeing me uncomfortable. Jeez. I should have never confessed that.

"It would have been nice if it was you, yes," I say at last, not wanting to let him win. Let him turn red for a while.

But he doesn't blush. He just looks thoughtful.

"Anyway," he says, apparently wimping out and changing the subject. "You're probably wondering why I asked you here tonight. And it wasn't, unfortunately, to dance with you."

"I figured," I say. "What's wrong?"

He picks up the salt shaker and fiddles with it, not meeting my eyes. "Kristoff," he murmurs at last.

I cock my head. "You mean your vamp friend? The one whose donors you saw in the Blood Bar yesterday?"

"Yes." Jareth nods. "I went to see him this evening. To let him know we'd spotted his donors and that he ought to let them go. I pounded on the door of his crypt, but there was no answer. I waited for a moment, then heard strange noises coming from inside. A . . . whimpering almost. So I broke down the door. I found him in bed, looking deathly ill."

Concern claws at my heart. I'm thinking, "This is very strange."

"I asked him what was wrong. He could barely speak." Jareth shakes his head, looking pained. Evidently this guy is a good friend. "He says the last few days, he's been bedridden. Can't even feed anymore. And all his vampire powers seem to somehow have left him."

"That's weird."

"Very. I've never seen anything like it."

"Do you think he could have caught some weird disease? Like, because his donors were at the Blood Bar? Maybe they were infected by some other vampire and passed along the disease."

Jareth shrugs. "It's possible, to be sure. But unlikely. The Blood Bar is more regulated than one might think. It screens all its biters. I had to go through a rigorous blood test before I was accepted into the program."

"So you think the two things are totally separate? Unrelated?"

"I wouldn't go that far. It's too much of a coincidence. Oh, and even stranger? His donors are dead."

My mouth drops open in horror. "Dead?"

Jareth nods.

"But we just saw them two nights ago. I mean, sure they looked a bit on the pasty side, but . . . dead?" Suddenly this was getting pretty scary.

"Dead." Jareth repeats. "And no one has any idea why."

"Couldn't they do an autopsy?"

"We could, but the humans have them, obviously. I sent some of my men to do recon and they learned that the girls' parents are doing their own autopsy. And, unfortunately, they're both going to be cremated immediately afterwards. So we can't get to their bodies."

"What would you need to find out what was wrong with them?"

"A sample of blood would probably do it. We have some talented chemists in our coven."

An idea forms in my mind. "Do you know what funeral home they've been sent to? We could maybe sneak in and get the sample or something."

Jareth raises an eyebrow. "You want to do that?" he asks. "It could be dangerous."

"I laugh in the face of danger," I quip, letting out a loud fake chortle. "Ha, ha, ha, ha!"

Jareth shakes his head, not able to suppress a small grin. Heh. Even he cannot resist Silly Rayne.

"Well, it's not a bad idea. I'm told the bodies are at the funeral home. But they haven't been worked on yet, so they still have their blood. We could go there before the place closes and hide out until after hours. Then we can get the blood sample."

"Sounds like a plan, Stan."

We leave Club Fang and head into the parking lot. Jareth suggests we take his black BMW and obviously I don't argue. Leather seats and satellite radio set to an all-Goth, all-the-time satellite station is my preferred way to travel. We drive to the outskirts of town, to the funeral home. Neither of us say much in the car, but it's a comfortable silence as Peter Murphy croons over the airwaves.

The funeral home is still open when we arrive. Dozens of cars are parked out front. Whoever's having a wake tonight was obviously pretty popular. I wonder how many people would come to my funeral. Luckily, if I turn vamp I'll get to fake my death and see for myself.

My dad better show up or he's so dead. And when he does die, I won't attend *his* funeral, just to spite him. Not that he'd be expecting me to, seeing as technically I'd have been the first to die.

The vampire stuff can get confusing at times. . . .

Jareth parks the car and suggests we go around to the other side of the house. The backyard hasn't gotten the same landscaping attention the front has and we have to push through tangled briar patches to get there, totally ripping up my tights. It's worth the fishnet sacrifice, though, when we find an unlocked window and slip inside.

"Let's find a closet or something to hide out in until the place closes for the night and the funeral guys go home," Jareth suggests.

"Okay." I feel like a guest star on *Six Feet Under*.

We tiptoe out into the hallway and try a couple doors. The first leads to a bathroom and the second to a tiny darkened chapel. (Which would have been the perfect place to hide were it not for the fact that Jareth's feet would pretty much burn off walking on hallowed ground.) Finally, on the third try, we find what we're looking for. A small broom closet filled with cleaning supplies that we'll both fit in.

Barely.

We squeeze in and Jareth pulls the door closed behind us. It's dark. There's no room to sit down and I pray that the wake is nearly over. Jareth's leg brushes against mine, sending a whole host of tingling sensations through my body. Did I happen to mention how hot he is? Half of me totally wants to jump him. Let him take me, right here, right now. I have to keep reminding myself I don't want him. I really don't want him.

"Are you okay?" Jareth whispers. "You're shaking."

Ugh. I'm shaking 'cause he's totally turning me on. But I can't exactly tell him that, now can I? At the same time, the last thing I want to do is let him think I'm scared.

"Low blood sugar," I whisper. "I only had an apple for lunch." I actually had four slices of pizza with extra cheese, but he doesn't need to know that.

"Sorry," he says. "We should have stopped at the drive-thru on the way. Sometimes I forget what it's like to be human. To have feeding needs."

"What about you? You have feeding needs, too, right? But I've never see you with your donors."

He grimaces. "I don't like the idea of donors. I get my blood by mail order."

I raise an eyebrow. Interesting. "Really? Why?"

"Would you like seeing the cow before eating your steak?"

"Uh, no. But I'm a vegetarian. No cows for this chick."

Jareth chuckles softly, the dim light catching his fangs and making them sparkle. "How are you going to become a vampire if you don't like the taste of blood?"

Good question. One I hadn't really given much thought to. "I figure I'll learn to love it," I say with a shrug. "Sunny was totally grossed out by the idea of drinking blood until she actually tasted it. Then she developed an unquenchable thirst for the stuff."

"I see. Well, then I'm sure you'll be fine," Jareth says. "So have they told you who will be your blood mate yet?"

"No. After the whole Sunny mishap, I'm back at the bottom of the waiting list. Which sucks, pardon the pun. You'd think Magnus, being the master and all, could pull in a few favors for his girlfriend's sister, but evidently not."

"Maybe it's because they haven't found you a perfect match yet," Jareth says. "Remember, your DNA has to be compatible."

"Yeah, I know. Knowing me, there will never be another vamp with compatible DNA. I'll be doomed to be a slayer for eternity."

"That's not true. They'll find you a match. Actually I think you'd make a good vamp," Jareth says shyly. "Though perhaps a very stubborn, aggravating blood mate."

"Heh." I laugh. "So what's your story? You on the prowl for a blood mate of your own?" As I ask the question, I suddenly realize I'm worried about his answer. For some reason, I really, really don't want him to say yes.

He's silent for a long moment, then says, "I don't want a blood mate. They offered me one a few years back, but I refused."

"But why?" I ask. "I thought that was every vampire's dream. To have a partner to spend eternity with."

"Eternity is a long time and it doesn't always work out that way," Jareth says, a bit bitterly. "It's worse to love someone and then lose them, then to never love at all."

"Heh. I know the feeling."

"Oh?"

I feel my face heat. I hadn't meant to be so revealing.

"Ah, nothing," I stammer. "It's just . . . my dad. He took off four years ago to find himself. Haven't seem him since."

"And you miss him," Jareth says softly. It's not a question. Or a judgment. Or even pity.

"Well, yeah. I mean, sure I do. Sometimes. Though sometimes I don't." I know I'm not making a lot of sense, but I'm not really used to talking about this stuff. Especially not to a hot vampire in a broom closet. "But anyway, I guess it doesn't matter now. He's coming for our birthday this week. So I mean, I guess it's all good." I pause, feeling awkward and not knowing what to say.

"Yes. That seems very good," Jareth says, a bit distantly.

"What about you? What's your story?" I ask, so ready to change the subject. "What makes you such a bitter biter?"

"It was a long time ago. It doesn't matter now."

Hm. Stubborn. But I'll get it out of him. "It obviously does. It obviously upsets you. Maybe it'd feel good to talk about it. To a stranger."

"A stranger like you?"

"Sure. I can't say I'll be able to give wise advice, but I'd be happy to listen. And we've got time."

"But you're a slayer."

"Dude. I'm like a good slayer—"

Jareth suddenly puts a hand over my mouth. I stop talking and listen. Footsteps. Coming closer. Shit. I hope the cleaning crew doesn't need to get into the broom closet. We'll totally be caught!

I look up at Jareth questioningly, having no idea what to do. His eyes are wide and frightened.

"Follow my lead," he whispers.

And then he leans down and kisses me!!!

Uh, sorry, have to continue this later. Mom's totally yelling at me to get to bed. . . .

**POSTED BY RAYNE McDONALD @ 1 A.M.**
**TWO COMMENTS:**

**CandyGrrl says . . .**
He kissed u!?!?! How can u leave us hanging like this? Tell ur mom this is more important! Gah!

**Soulsearcher says . . .**
Making out in a funeral home. Sooo romantic. Oh, so romantic.

**SunshineBaby says . . .**
You kissed Jareth? Dude, I'm your twin! How come I'm always the last to know?

# 17

## Closet Kisses and a Lot of Wishes

Quick entry before school since you're all annoyed that I had to cut out at the kissing scene. Believe me, I didn't want to leave you hanging either, but Mom was being totally adamant. I think she's still pissed that we scared off her date. Oh, and speaking of? I think she's still seeing the guy. Grrr. I've got to have a talk with her.

Anyway, where I left off: footsteps approaching and I'm getting ravaged by the sexiest vampire on earth. But forget the footsteps. You just want to know about the ravaging, right? Heh.

You know how I said how heavenly the bite from Jareth

was? Well, the kiss he gave me last night was even better, if you can believe it!

Here's how it went down:

His mouth captures mine. I know that sounds funny, but that's exactly what it seems like. Total domination of my lips. I'm so surprised that my jaw drops, which inadvertently allows him full access. And he takes advantage, his lips pressing hard against mine, his tongue finding my own and meeting it with almost a worshipful caress. Obviously it's hard to describe kisses, but think of your best kiss ever and multiply it by three and a half million and you're probably pretty close. Every nerve ending in my body is like, singing, at this point. Just like in romance books, there's, like, this electricity flowing through my veins. Suddenly I don't care why we're kissing or the fact that we're probably, like, this close to getting busted by whoever's coming to the closet. All I can think of, focus on, is his lips against mine.

Half of me wishes you could all kiss Jareth, just so you can feel for yourselves. The other half hopes that Jareth never kisses anyone else but me for the rest of eternity.

The footsteps fade and Jareth pulls away, way too soon for my liking.

"Sorry," he says, his normally pale face bright red. "I just figured if they caught us, it'd be better to look like we snuck off together, than were hiding for some other more nefarious purpose."

I nod, not trusting my voice at the moment. I'm madly praying the footsteps come back so we can go for round two. But I'm just not that lucky. Whoever it was hits the lights and slams the front door closed. They're out.

I involuntarily lick my lower lip, nearly desperate for another taste. So delicious. So, so delicious. My whole body is humming. I'm dying to just jump him. I wonder what he'd do if I did. Would he pull away? Be disgusted? Or does he feel the same attraction I do? I wish I knew.

We stand in silence, still so close that I can feel Jareth's cool breath on my face. I wonder for a moment why vampires need to breathe, seeing as they're technically not alive. I'll have to look it up later.

Five minutes go by. Then five more. It seems like an eternity. I wish, not for the first time, that we could kiss again. But Jareth seems to be stuck in full-on listening mode.

Finally he speaks.

"I think they're gone. We're safe," he says. He pushes open the door and puts a hand around the small of my back to lead me out into the hallway. Just that small touch sparks a thrill strong enough to curl my toes. I wonder what it'd be like to get it on with him for real. I probably wouldn't be able to handle it. Would he be rough and demanding? Or gentle, soft, and sweet? And what would he be like afterward? Would he want to cuddle? Or, like most of my past boyfriends, reach for the PlayStation controller, afterward. I'm so over those guys.

Guess I'll never know. And there's no use fantasizing about it, now is there?

Anyhow, we creep through the dark hallway, down the stairs, and into the basement. There, Jareth finds a hanging light and pulls the string, enveloping the room in a dim yellowy glow. I look around, my breath catching in my throat as I recognize what surrounds me.

Corpses. Everywhere I look. Freak-y. I've never seen dead bodies in real life before.

Of course, they don't seem to bother Jareth even the slightest. I guess that's probably because technically speaking he's a living, walking, breathing corpse himself. He heads straight over to the wall, where there's a large filing cabinet–like setup and starts reading the drawer labels. He pauses at one and then pulls open the drawer. Out pops (surprise, surprise) another body. Ugh. I'm so going to have nightmares tonight. This is worse than the time Spider and I had an all-night *Friday the 13th*–watching marathon. Every time I closed my eyes for weeks later I saw hockey-masked Jason lumbering up to me with his machete, ready to creatively murder me for my sex, drugs, and rock-and-roll sins.

"This is one of them," he says, motioning me over. "And she hasn't been drained yet. Excellent." He reaches into his black leather trench coat pocket (way cool) and pulls out a small silver dagger, an empty vial, and a pair of rubber gloves, which he slips on his hands.

"Wait. You're not going to—" I start, stopping only when I realize indeed he is going to do just that. He draws a small slash across her arm and holds the vial underneath to catch the blood. I involuntarily cringe.

He looks up and laughs when he sees my face. "Relax, dear," he says. "She can't feel it. She's already dead."

"I know," I say, annoyed, but more at myself than at him. Some super vampire-chick-in-training I'm turning out to be—afraid of a little blood. What's going to happen when I have to dine on it every night? Maybe I'll do what Jareth does and get takeout. At least that way I can pretend it's wine or something. Though it sort of takes all the romance out of the process.

The vial fills quickly and Jareth plugs it with a small rubber stopper. Then he reaches into his pocket again and pulls out a small cloth, which he presses against the open wound. "To stop the blood," he explains.

"Don't want her to bleed to death, eh?" I quip.

He grins. "Definitely not," he says. "Not to mention the smell of the stuff is driving me crazy. It's taking everything I've got not to lean down and take a sip."

"You'd better not. We don't know what's in that stuff. What if she is the reason Kristoff's out of commission?"

"Exactly. That would be . . . as you humans say . . . so not cool." He says it in a total valley girl voice, causing me to giggle. He really can be funny when he's not being a jerk.

"I'm glad I can make you laugh," he says with a small smile and I totally feel my face going beet red. I have no idea how to respond to him, but luckily it turns out I don't have to. A moment later he removes the cloth and examines the corpse's wound. "Okay," he says. "Let's get out of this place."

We leave the funeral home and Jareth drops me off at my place. The good-bye scene is très awkward for some reason. As if neither of us really wants to part company. And as if both of us want a goodnight kiss when we do. Unfortunately, we're both total chickens and instead of confessing our desires we stumble over our goodnights with much stammering and blushing and I get out of the car and head for the house.

And that's about it. Time for (sigh) me to head to school. TTYL.


**POSTED BY RAYNE McDONALD @ 8 A.M.**
**ONE COMMENT:**


**NotYourMama says . . .**
Wow, that sounds like quite the kiss, girl! I would love to get me some of that. You let us know if you decide he's not the guy for you and I'll be all over that *sheeyat*.

# 18

## Gamer Girls

After school I go to my room and sign on to my video game. Spider and I are supposed to join our fellow guild members to do an instance. For those of you who think I'm speaking some other language when I go all gamer geek, a "guild" is a group of friends who play together online and an "instance" is like a special dungeon in the game where your characters can kill computer-generated monsters for really good treasure. (If you still don't get it, ask your brother or boyfriend. They probably play and will be overjoyed to go off on a way-too-detailed explanation that you'll get bored of after about half a minute.)

Anyway—Spider and I had a long chat about Jareth while we played.

Pasting the transcript here. The stuff in "whisper" is Spider and my private convo.

**KELAHDKA:** Everyone in? We ready to start?

**RAYNIEDAY:** Yup.

**SPIDER:** Yup.

**RUKKU:** Yup.

**HAXOR:** Yup.

**KELAHDKA:** Okay, here's the plan. . . .

**SPIDER WHISPERS:** So how's everything going with the whole slayer thing? You kill the bad guy yet? Save the world?

**RAYNIEDAY WHISPERS:** No. ☹ Not yet. But something weird is definitely going on. Some donor girls who visited the Blood Bar died after infecting their vampire with some kind of weird blood disease.

**SPIDER WHISPERS:** That doesn't seem so good.

**RAYNIEDAY WHISPERS:** Watch out!

*\*\*Spider firebombs Acolyte for 40 damage.*

*\*\*Scarlet Monastary Acolyte hits Spider for 450 damage.*

**SPIDER:** Uh, can I get a heal?

**SPIDER:** Anyone? Hax?

**HAXOR:** Hang on. I'm on the phone.

*\*\*Scarlet Monastary Acolyte hits Spider for 230 damage.*
*\*\*Spider dies.*

**SPIDER WHISPERS:** Grr. He did that on purpose.

**RAYNIEDAY WHISPERS:** ☹

**SPIDER WHISPERS:** It's 'cause I broke up with him, you know. Ever since I broke up with him I never get healed when we're playing.

**RAYNIEDAY WHISPERS:** You're imagining things. Why would he not heal you? It only delays the whole group. Surely he's not that stupid.

**SPIDER WHISPERS:** He is that stupid. He totally is. Why do you think I dumped him?

**HAXOR:** Sorry. Back. Oh, Spider, you're dead?

**SPIDER:** . . .

**RAYNIEDAY WHISPERS:** Be nice.

**SPIDER:** Why, yes, Hax. I died. How sweet of you to take time out of your busy real life to notice.

**RAYNIEDAY WHISPERS:** Uh, when I said nice . . .

**SPIDER WHISPERS:** Forget him. Tell me more about the vamps.

**RAYNIEDAY WHISPERS:** Hehe. I've got MAJOR scoop actually.

**SPIDER WHISPERS:** Oh?

**RAYNIEDAY WHISPERS:** . . . I kissed Jareth!!!!

**SPIDER:** OMG, YOU KISSED HIM!?!

**SPIDER:** Uh, mistype.

**HAXOR:** Who kissed who?

**SPIDER:** I said MISTYPE. As in I didn't mean to type it to you. So eff off.

*\*\*HaxOr cries.*
*\*\*Rukku comforts HaxOr.*

**SPIDER WHISPERS:** God, this party sucks.

**KELAHDKA:** Okay, we're going to attack the boss now. Here's the strategy. . . .

**SPIDER WHISPERS:** Anyway, you kissed him? Why did you kiss him? I thought you hated him. Or at least thought he was annoying.

**RAYNIEDAY WHISPERS:** Well, it wasn't like a real kiss. I mean, we were in this broom closet and . . .

**SPIDER WHISPERS:** Broom closet? OMG, how sexy is that?!

**RAYNIEDAY WHISPERS:** Uh, at a funeral home . . .

**SPIDER WHISPERS:** A Goth's dream come true.

**RAYNIEDAY WHISPERS:** And someone was coming. We were afraid they were going to open the door. . . .

**SPIDER WHISPERS:** . . .

**RAYNIEDAY WHISPERS:** And so he kissed me. So we'd look like we snuck away from the wake or something if caught.

**SPIDER WHISPERS:** And . . .

**RAYNIEDAY WHISPERS:** And what?

**SPIDER WHISPERS:** Don't play coy with me, young lady. What was it like?

**RAYNIEDAY WHISPERS:** /blush

**SPIDER WHISPERS:** LOL.


**KELAHDKA:** Okay, here we go! Spider, go ahead and fireball these guys. Hax will keep you healed.

**SPIDER:** kk.


**SPIDER WHISPERS:** I want to hear more after this battle.


*\*\*Spider firebombs Scarlet Henchman for 400 damage.*


**HAXOR:** Uh, my dog's scratching at the door. I'll BRB.

**SPIDER:** Wait, I already attacked!


*\*\*Scarlet Henchman attacks Spider for 430 damage.*
*\*\*Scarlet Hound of Hell attacks Spider for 200 damage.*

*\*\*Scarlet Priest attacks Spider for 235 damage.*
*\*\*Scarlet Rogue attacks Spider for 500 damage.*
*\*\*Spider dies.*


**SPIDER:** GDAMNIT, HAX!

**HAXOR:** Okay. Sorry I'm back. Oh, Spider. You're dead again?

**SPIDER WHISPERS:** Worst priest ever.

**RAYNIEDAY WHISPERS:** Sigh.

**SPIDER WHISPERS:** That's it. I'm logging out. I can't take it.

**RAYNIEDAY WHISPERS:** But don't you want to hear the rest of the kiss?

**SPIDER WHISPERS:** Oh, yeah. Okay. One more try. But so help me if he doesn't heal me again.

**RAYNIEDAY WHISPERS:** kk.

**SPIDER WHISPERS:** You can tell me what the kiss was like while my ghost runs back to my dead body.

**RAYNIEDAY WHISPERS:** Well, it was the most amazing kiss in the entire history of kissing. Like in that movie *Princess Bride* where they talk about best-ever kisses? This had to be one of them.

**SPIDER WHISPERS:** That good, huh?

**RAYNIEDAY WHISPERS:** Yes. Majorly dreamy. You know, Spider, I hate to admit this, but I think I might be in love.

**SPIDER WHISPERS:** What? With Jareth?

**RAYNIEDAY WHISPERS:** He seems all cold on the outside, but he's kind of sweet on the inside. And easy to talk to and stuff.

**SPIDER WHISPERS:** But he's a vampire.

**RAYNIEDAY WHISPERS:** So what? My sis is dating a vampire.

**SPIDER WHISPERS:** Your sis is not a vampire slayer. And besides, the guy sounds kind of emotionally unavailable.

**RAYNIEDAY WHISPERS:** Emotionally unavailable? WTF? You suddenly Freud or something?

**SPIDER WHISPERS:** No. Freud was the "He reminds me of my father" guy.

**RAYNIEDAY WHISPERS:** Well, Jareth definitely does not remind me of my father.

**SPIDER WHISPERS:** Are you sure about that? From what you've told me he sounds like he's another guy who won't share his feelings or get close to anyone for fear he'll become trapped.

**RAYNIEDAY WHISPERS:** Jareth isn't like that. I know he's not. He's just been hurt and now he's afraid.

**SPIDER WHISPERS:** But what is this big hurt?

**RAYNIEDAY WHISPERS:** I don't know. But I'm going to find out.

**SPIDER WHISPERS:** Okay, sweetie. Good luck. Just don't get hurt, okay?

**RAYNIEDAY WHISPERS:** I'll try.

*\*\*Spider resurrects.*

**SPIDER:** Okay, I'm back.

**KELAHDKA:** Great. We're going to try this again. Spider, you attack and we'll cover you.

**SPIDER:** Uh, Hax, you're going to heal me this time, right?

**HAXOR:** Of course. What are you talking about? Why wouldn't I?

**SPIDER:** Okay, never mind. Here goes.

*\*\*Spider attacks Scarlet Henchman for 300 damage.*

**HAXOR:** Oh. My friend just got here. I've got to go.

*\*\*HaxOr leaves the party.*
*\*\*Scarlet Henchman attacks Spider for 100 damage.*
*\*\*Scarlet Demon Dog attacks Spider for 245 damage.*
*\*\*Scarlet Rogue attacks Spider for 567 damage.*
*\*\*Spider dies.*

**SPIDER:** NOOOOO!!!!!!!!!

**POSTED BY RAYNE McDONALD @ 12 A.M.**
**EIGHT COMMENTS:**

**HaxOr says . . .**
Dude! That's bogus that I don't heal Spider. She gets healed plenty. She's just such a crappy noob mage she gets pwned anyway. I demand you take this libelous slander out of your blog before I sue you for everything you got.

**Spider says . . .**
First of all, Hax, it's obviously apparent from that transcript that it is YOU who are the noob! Also, what the hell do you mean, sue? You can't sue someone over a video game chat. Grow up and get a life.

**HaxOr says . . .**
I have a life, thank you very much. A life WITHOUT YOU.

**Spider says . . .**
There is no life after me. Heh. Heh.

**HaxOr says . . .**
U R A STUPID BITCH.

**Spider says . . .**
U R A PATHETIC A-HOLE.

**Hax0r says . . .**

That's it! Now I'm going to sue you, too, Spider!!!!!

**Rayne says . . .**

Hax0r! Spider! Get your own blogs and stop fighting in mine! I mean it.

# 19

## BIRTHDAY GRRL!!!!

Yay! Today is my birthday!!!! How exciting!!!! Yes, I know I'm exclamation-pointing too much, but you would be, too, if it were your birthday!!!!

First Mom's going to cook a birthday breakfast—and she's promised to make real pancakes without any tofu, barley, or carrots in them. Extra unhealthy with whipped cream and strawberries.

In the afternoon, Spider's coming over, as are various friends of Sunny's. Mom's going to order pizza and we Netflixed a bunch of DVDs. Of course, Sunny's selection will probably have all Matthew McConaughey stuff. But I rented some classics. The original *Dracula*, starring Bela Lugosi for one. Can't wait!

But what I'm most excited about is Dad. I can't believe he's actually coming. I haven't seen him in so many years. I'm so proud of Sunny for getting up the courage to write to him and invite him. I would have never been able to do that.

I wonder what he'll look like. If he's started to gray at his temples. Will he look old? Or maybe just distinguished? I wonder what he'll bring us for presents. I don't even care if he does, actually. Just having him here is present enough.

Ooh, this is going to be the best day, ever! I *sooo* cannot wait for it to begin.

Oops, Mom's calling me to breakfast and I haven't even selected a b-day outfit yet. Gah! Better get a move on. . . .

**POSTED BY RAYNE McDONALD @ 7 A.M.**
**THREE COMMENTS:**

**ButterfliQT says . . .**
Happy birthday, sweetie! Enjoy the time with your dad.

**DarkGothBoy says . . .**
Happy Birthday 2 u
Happy Birthday 2 u

U look like a vampire
& U smell like one, too.

**Spider says . . .**
See you this afternoon. Can't wait to meet the dadster.

# 20

## NO CAKE

t's ten o'clock. He's still not here. Sunny and my mom have gone to bed. I'm sitting downstairs on the family computer, surrounded by leftover pizza, stupid presents I don't want or need, and NO CAKE.

I hate him.

I HATE HIM.

I HATE HATE HATE HATE HATE HATE HATE HIM!!!!!

**POSTED BY RAYNE McDONALD @ 10 P.M.**
**FOUR COMMENTS:**

Anonymous says . . .
Oh, he didn't show up? What a surprise. Poor Raynie. Now she's really going to have daddy issues. Boo-hoo-hoo. The Goth freak suffers some more. Maybe you should go listen to Morrissey and slit your wrists.

Anonymous says . . .
Ha-ha! I could have predicted that.

Anonymous says . . .
Oh, the teenage angst. Makes me a little sick. Welcome to the real world, little one.

Anonymous says . . .
Maybe this will teach you to stop playing your little vampire games and face reality a bit, sweetheart.

# 21

## My Dad's a Loser and I Think He Should Die

*Dear Diary,*
*I used to write a blog and post it on the Internet. But let me tell you, it's not fun posting about your life when bad things happen and then have anonymous people post nasty, hurtful comments about you. So screw that. I'm going to stick with a good old-fashioned lock-and-key diary from now on.*

Anyway, it's Sunday afternoon. Not that it matters. I don't think I would have gotten out of bed even if I did have school. I'm such a moron. I actually stayed up waiting for the guy 'til one A.M. As if he'd suddenly come through the door at one A.M., arms full of presents and cake, mouth full of apologies for being late.

Obviously that didn't happen. Not that I really expected it would. Not really, anyway.

Did I mention I hate him?

Screw this. That was his last chance. I am never speaking to him again. Not in a thousand years. A million if I end up turning into a vamp and happen to live that long. He's already dead to me. If I came upon his grave somewhere in my vampirish travels I'd spit on it.

I hate him, I hate him, I HATE HIM!!!!

I'm such an idiot. Why did I buy Sunny's crap about him definitely coming? About how it has to be real 'cause there's a plane ticket and a hotel? Last night I called the airport. The hotel. He just never showed up. Stood them up, just like he did us.

Bastard. Effing bastard.

I wish I could just jump on a plane and head straight to his house and confront him in person. Tell him what a lousy father he is and how he doesn't deserve good daughters like Sunny and me. Or something. Anything. Just so I don't have to feel so freaking helpless and screwed up and alone.

Great. Now I'm crying again and I'm so not a crying type of girl. This whole thing sucks. I don't have time to be all depressed either. I've got Slayer Training scheduled at two, if you can believe it. Teifert called me this morning (Does the entire world know my cell number?), leaving a cryptic message about the time growing near. Which is fine by me, I suppose.

I'm more than ready to kick a little ass.

# 22

## Stake That!

Back from Slayer Training. Definitely a mind-blowing experience, let me tell you.

At first everything seems pretty normal. Mr. Teifert and I meet up in the school gymnasium, down by the weight room. The place is deserted, which is probably a good thing. A student and a teacher, alone in a half-lit gym—probably a bit sketchy-looking to your average outsider. And it's not like we can explain the whole slayer/instructor thing to the general public. They're bound to make up a much seedier scenario—one that will get Teifert fired and me expelled. Not so good.

Oh, but get this! Mr. Teifert forces me to change into a pair of Juicy Couture sweatpants and Nikes before starting my training. Says something about my beautiful black silk dress and combat boots combo not being appropriate work-out attire. *Puh-leeze*. Oh, and if that wasn't bad enough—this pair of Juicy Couture sweatpants just so happens to be pink! If anyone evil and cruel were to walk by with a camera phone at this very moment, my entire high school image would be ir-reparably shattered.

After donning the Pepto-Bismol outfit, we start our training. He has me do some weight lifting first (five pounds is about my limit) and then jump rope (three jumps maybe before I get hopelessly tangled), then run laps around the gymnasium. (And when I say laps, I mean lap—singular—before I'm completely out of breath. I've so got to give up smoking.)

He looks a little distraught at my physical condition, but simply motions to the punching bag and tells me to go at it. I smile. Now we're talking.

"Hi-YAH!" I cry as I slam my fist into the punching bag and then follow it with a beautiful roundhouse kick. I lower my head and narrow my eyes and focus on the bag, making it my enemy. If I'm lucky, this Slayer Training will get some of my pent-up aggression out.

Dad. Is. A. Loser. Punch. Kick. Repeat.

"Rayne, focus. You're not in control," Teifert repeats for the ten-thousandth time. "A slayer must find her deep strength. Her inner power. She must become one with the universe."

I stop punching, reaching up to wipe the sweat from my forehead. "Can we cut the Zen crap for a moment?" I ask. "I'm trying to beat this bag to a pulp."

"No we cannot cut the 'Zen crap' as you say," Teifert says wearily. "Rayne, one cannot become a good slayer through sheer force and anger. You must find the power within your center. Within yourself."

"Maybe I don't have a center. And if so, maybe I should use what I got." I hold up my fists. "Here's where my power lies, Teifert. Look out, vamps, it's Raynie Power time."

Teifert shakes his head. "Where do they find these girls?" he mutters under his breath. "And why do they keep sending them to me?"

Oh, that's nice. "Hey, you chose me, dude," I remind him, lowering my fists. "I didn't ask for this gig." Great, now I'm a slayer reject, too. Go figure. I punch the bag a few more times. Might as well burn some calories while he's bemoaning my slayer suckiness. "Maybe you chose wrong. Ever think about that? Maybe I'm not really slayer material."

"We don't choose wrong. We have a very precise methodology for picking our slayers. You just don't see the power you have. You're stubborn and you refuse to learn. And therefore your power will remain dormant. Locked inside of you."

He grabs the punching bag so it no longer sways with my hits. "Let's try you with your stake."

He motions over to the bench, where I left the half-carved chunk of wood. I roll my eyes.

"Can't I get a real weapon?" I whine, walking over to the stake and picking it up with some reluctance. "A sword maybe? Or a big two-handed axe like Buffy?"

"By carving this stake, you have embedded it with your slayer essence," Teifert explains, completely ignoring my request for sharp metal objects of death. "Now, it has bonded itself to you and will only work when wielded by your hand. Each stake is unique to its slayer."

"Sort of like the wands in *Harry Potter*?" I can't help but ask.

"When you take this weapon into your hands, you will feel the essence of the tree from which it was taken. You will be filled with the power of that mighty oak. The strength will flow through you and make you one with Mother Earth. Only then will you be able to find your center. And get the job done."

"Huh." I roll the stake around in my palm. "And to think this looks like something you grabbed out in the schoolyard."

"Hold up the stake, Rayne," Teifert commands. "And concentrate on its power."

I sigh, then do what I'm told. Otherwise I'll probably be here all day. I raise the stake above my head and focus my eyes on it.

And then things start to get weird.

As I stare at the stake, the world around me starts to lose focus and the wood starts to take on an almost unearthly glow. I watch in awe as it morphs right before my eyes from a chunk of unpolished wood into a sleek, sharp instrument, smooth as glass. I wave it around, hesitantly at first, then with growing assurance. So cool. So, so cool. I wish you could have seen it.

"Am I making it do that?" I whisper. From the corner of my eye I can see Teifert's nod.

"You are the chosen one. The slayer. As I said, we don't make mistakes."

"Wow, that's pretty amazing." I step forward, toward the punching bag, and then stab the wood into it, with all my might. The stake slides through the tough leather like a knife through butter. Whoa! Now we're talking.

I pull the stake out. It's no longer glowing. I turn to Teifert. "Okay, I believe you now," I say. "Who knew I had all this power in me?"

"Who knew you were going to stab the punching bag?" Teifert grumbles, not looking at all impressed by my feat. He walks over to the bag and examines the hole. "Do you know how expensive these things are to replace?"

"Dude! I've just been given magical superpowers to slay vamps and all you care about is your Visa bill?"

Teifert turns back to me. "So you believe now? That with your stake you have the power to slay vampires?"

"Hell yeah, I believe. Just call me Raynie: Vampire Slayer. Able to kill vampires in a single bound." I wave my stake around again, but it fails to light up this time. I'm probably not concentrating hard enough. Gotta remember that when the zero hour comes around.

"Good. I'd like to have additional training sessions with you, but I'm not sure there's time," Teifert says. "How have your investigations into Maverick been going? Have you learned anything?"

"Well, sort of, though we definitely need more info before some conviction," I say hesitantly. "There seems to be some kind of disease going around. We saw some donors of a high-ranking vampire in the Blood Coven at the bar one night—"

Teifert raises an eyebrow. "We? Are you working with someone? It's highly irregular for a slayer to have a partner."

I roll my eyes. "Uh, what about Buffy? She had that whole Scooby gang on her side and that didn't seem to hurt her odds."

"Repeat after me, Rayne. Buffy. Is. A. TV. Character. She. Is. Not. Real."

Sigh. "Look. If you must know, I'm working with one of Magnus's guys. General Jareth. Don't worry, he's on our side. After all, the vamps want to know what's going down at the Blood Bar as much as we do."

"Jareth, huh?" Teifert says thoughtfully. "I think I

remember reading about him. He caused some trouble for Slayer Inc. back in the day."

"Trouble?" Oh, great. Me and my big mouth. What if they suddenly want me to dust Jareth? I could never do that. I wonder if this has something to do with whatever secret Jareth is hiding. . . .

"Never mind. It's all in the past, anyhow," Teifert says with a dismissive wave. "So fine, you're working with Jareth. And what have you two found?"

"Okay, like I was saying, one night we saw those two donors of a high-ranking coven guy and the next day those same donors turned up dead. And their vampire, Kristoff, is weak and sick and has lost most of his powers. I mean, it could be unrelated, but . . ."

Teifert scratches his chin. "Interesting," he muses. "Perhaps Maverick is trying a less direct approach to infiltrate the coven."

"What do you mean?"

"What if he were somehow infecting the donors purposefully? So they could bring the disease back to their masters. By weakening the inner core of Magnus's coven, a takeover could more easily be accomplished."

"Wow. That's pretty elaborate."

"These vampires have thousands of years to plot this kind of thing. They can afford to come up with detailed plans because there's no need to rush."

"I guess that's true."

"So what do you plan to do next?"

"Well, Jareth and I took a sample of the donor's blood and he's having it analyzed in the lab now."

"That's something, I suppose. But what we really need is a sample of the virus itself," Teifert says. "You should go down to the Blood Bar and find out where they store these viruses and bring one back to me. Hopefully this way we can develop an antidote before too many vampires are infected and Maverick is able to stage his coup."

"Uh, yeah, sure. That should be easy." I make a face, in case he can't hear the total sarcasm in my voice. "I'm sure they'll be happy to let me borrow one, once I show my library card."

"Rayne, you are the slayer. Vampires fear you, not the other way around. Just bring your stake with you. It gives you your power. With it, you'll easily be able to defeat anyone who stands in your way."

"Okay, okay. Stake will be at arm's reach at all times." I tuck the chunk of wood into the back of my sweatpants. "Just like this, but with a much classier outfit." Could you imagine me wearing Juicy Couture down to the Blood Bar?

"Rayne, this is serious business," Teifert scolds. "Do not take your duties lightly. If Maverick is to take control of the Blood Coven, he could conceivably unite the vampires against the humans and start a war. A war that mankind is unlikely to win."

Nice, huh? Talk about putting on the pressure. The fate of the world lies in my hands. Suddenly I feel very weary and depressed.

# 23

## Mike Stevens Must Die

Monday. Did I ever mention how much I hate my school? Well, not the school itself. I've got nothing against the bricks or mortar or climbing ivy. It's the cretins that inhabit it that make me want to slit my wrists on a daily basis.

For one thing, everyone's a clone of everyone else. All the girls with their flat-ironed hair, baby doll T's, and low, low-rise jeans. And the guys—they literally have no idea other clothing stores besides Abercrombie and Fitch even exist.

My friend River and her parents moved away to Boston a year ago. She says there are tons of cool skaters and Goths at her new school. That everyone's open-minded and there aren't really any cliques. Here at Oakridge, we've got nothing but cliques. And certainly no Goths besides me. So I'm the designated freak, basically, and everyone knows it.

It's a lonely life, but it's still better than shopping at American Eagle.

I usually don't care. In fact, if anything, I've always enjoyed being unique. An individual. But today feels different for some reason. Instead of mocking the cheerleaders who stride through the corridors in giggling packs, or the lovebirds who press against the lockers, making out and hoping the teachers won't walk by, or the jocks who "go long," passing the football to one another down the hallways, I notice myself envying them all. They look so blissful. So content in their pathetic, shallow high school existence.

And I, I realize suddenly, am totally and utterly alone. I can put on a brave front, ridicule them, whatever, but at the end of the day I'm the one who's the joke. Because they're happy and I'm not. They're free and I've got the weight of the world on my shoulders. All this time I've thought myself superior to them, but really I'm more pathetic.

As I walk down the hall, I feel the stares of the other students burning into my backside. They're laughing at me. They think I'm a weirdo. A loser. And I hate to say it, but maybe they're right. I mean, my own father doesn't even think I'm worthy of a birthday cake. And he was there at my conception.

Anger churns deep in my gut. I harden my face to match

their stares, forcing myself not to cry. Screw them all. I don't need them. I don't need Dad. I don't need anyone.

And then I run into Mike Stevens.

I hate Mike Stevens more than anyone at my school. If I'm the designated freak, he's the designated golden boy. Captain of the varsity football team, even though he's a junior. Student body president. Ash blond hair and sparkling green eyes. And a cocky smile that says he knows he's worshipped by half the school and feels he deserves everything life's dished him.

When we were in elementary school and everyone was like everyone else and there were no cliques, Mike Stevens and I used to play in the mud together at recess. When we were six, he kissed me.

That was a long time ago. We don't bring that up much. Actually, ever. In fact, I'm not sure he even remembers, which is probably a good thing.

These days we'd rather hurl mud at each other than play in it. And today he had the perfect weapon. My hickey.

It's not a hickey, of course. It's a bite mark from a vampire. But that's not something I can convince Mike of, obviously. Sigh. I thought the mark had faded enough to stop wearing a turtleneck, but evidently not.

"Hey, my little Goth princess," Golden Boy says to me after first period, leaning against the row of lockers. I pull out my books and stuff them into my black book bag, trying to ignore him, even though he's positioned himself directly in my line of sight. He's all cargo pants and Patriots jerseyed out as usual. "Who's the lucky guy?"

"Not you, that's for sure." I growl. I am so not in the mood for this today of all days. Not when I already feel so lousy about life, the universe, and everything.

He laughs. "Of course not. I don't do freaks."

"Good. Because I don't do Muggles."

At first I think he may miss the literary reference, but evidently even this illiterate fool has read *Harry Potter*. Those books are just way too popular. I may have to give them up for something more obscure.

"So, witch, which warlock gave you the hickey then?"

"It's not a hickey."

"Oh, really," he says sarcastically. "What, did you burn yourself with a curling iron like Mary Markson seems to do every Monday morning?"

Mary Markson and her boyfriend, Nick, have been going out for eons. They're totally most likely to get married. And she does have a tendency to show up to school with a lot of unsavory neck bruises. She insists she's just clumsy with the curling iron, but since she never has any actual curls to back up the claim, we're all a bit doubtful.

"No. Not a curling iron burn. I got bit by a vampire if you must know."

He rolls his eyes. I knew I was safe to say that. He'd never believe me in a million years. "Ah. So that's your type. I should have guessed."

"No. You shouldn't have guessed. You shouldn't have even noticed. What, are you staring at me from across the halls now? Stalking me?" Ever since I humiliated him in seventh grade (don't ask) he's made it his life's mission to make mine a living hell. Sunny thinks he secretly has a crush on me. Which is just . . . ew.

Mike frowns. Evidently I've struck a nerve. "Please. Your hickey is so big Blind Mr. Bannon the Biology teacher could see it."

"Good. I want the whole world to see the bite of my dark lover."

Jareth is not, of course, my dark lover. Or even my light one. Or any kind of lover, unfortunately. (As much as I might want him to be.) But I can't exactly back down and let Mike win.

"So when do you turn into a vampire then?" the stupid jock queries.

"I'm not going to turn into a vampire, moron. I've just been bitten. I'd have to drink the blood of a vampire to turn into one. Duh. And they don't just let anyone do that. There's a waiting list."

"A waiting list? There's actually enough of you freaks out

there for a waiting list?" He bends over, hands on knees, and laughs and laughs.

Grr. Did I mention I hate this guy? I notice a few students have stopped in the hallway, pretending to chat, but really wanting to take in the scene. The Goth girl against the jock boy. It's good reality programming. But I'm just not in the mood.

"Dude, don't you have some cheerleaders to seduce or beer to chug? Some nerd to copy off of? I know your life's lame and all, but certainly you must be able to think of a better way to waste it than talking to me."

He opens his mouth to reply, then I see him glance over at our audience. He seems to decide against what he was originally going to say and instead retorts, "Whatever skank," extra loud, to make sure everyone hears him insult me.

Then he hacks up a loogie and spits on me—ACTUALLY SPITS ON ME—before turning to walk away.

I'm so furious I don't even think. I just drop my books and my bag and run after him, slamming my entire body weight against his retreating back and managing to knock him off balance and onto the floor. My hands take on minds of their own as I punch and slap over and over as he struggles to get out from under me. But he's no match for my super slayer strength. If only I had my stake. I wonder if it works on Muggles.

The fight only lasts a minute or two before Monsieur Dawson, the French teacher, pulls me off of Mike.

"Arrêtez!" he commands. "Allez au bureau du principal!" The guy never speaks English. Which is kind of annoying for those of us who take Spanish. But in this case, even foreign-language-challenged me has a pretty good idea what he's saying.

"It's not my fault. She just jumped me. For no reason. Crazy freak!" Mike says, shooting me daggers.

Angrily I smooth out my skirt and glare back at Mike. Bastard. Now I've got detention and Mom's going to be so pissed at me.

"I'm going to get you for this, you skank freak," Mike adds as Monsieur Dawson drags him away. "Just you wait."

I sigh. I just wish I could somehow turn the guy into a vampire so I could stake him through the heart. Him and my father. The two of them should really die.

# 24

## Parents Just Don't Understand

So of course Mom totally freaks out about my detention. Especially since it was due to fighting. As you can imagine, as a hippie she's very into peace. And it's not just peace in the Middle East—that would at least be understandable. She evidently is advocating peace at Oakridge High as well. Puhleeze. If only she knew what an obnoxious jerk Mike Stevens is. I try to explain how he spit on me, but she starts spouting something about turning the other cheek. As if I want to get spit on my other cheek next time. Ew!

And the worst part is that she doesn't ground me, she wants to have a "talk." Ugh. I hate talks. I'd much rather be sent to my room without supper and kept there 'til I grow cobwebs. Locked in a tower like Rapunzel would suit me just fine. Just as long as I don't have to talk and share my feelings. (And, uh, grow my hair that long. I have a hard enough time with tangles as it is.)

"You've been acting very angry lately," she says, closing the door to my bedroom and joining me on the bed. I stare at my hands. This is so not fair. So, so not fair. "What's bothering you? Is it your father not showing up for your birthday?" she adds, in that horrible pity voice of hers. Grr. Nothing's worse than the pity voice.

"No," I retort. I knew she'd try that. Try to drag Dad into it.

"I know that must have hurt a lot, sweetie. I'm really sorry about that."

"I'm fine," I retort, anger welling up inside me, bubbling in my stomach, and making me feel sick. I knew we should have never told her about Dad's supposed plans to visit.

Mom frowns. "I don't think so, dear. People who are fine don't get into fights at school."

"They do if they're provoked by asshole football players."

Mom winces a bit at the swearing, but doesn't comment on it. "Are you having problems at school, Rayne?" she asks. "I've noticed your grades are slipping as well. You went from honor roll to C student this year."

"Yeah, well I have stupid teachers." Stupid teachers who always favor the jocks and cheerleaders. Stupid teachers who think just because I dress in black I'm doomed to be a dropout and don't give me the time of day. I'm smarter than all those losers I go to school with.

"What don't you like about them?"

Sigh. "Nothing. They're fine. Forget I said anything." The less I talk, the shorter this will take. I'm supposed to meet up with Spider and I can't leave Spider waiting.

"I don't want to forget you said anything. I want you to tell me what's wrong." Mom reaches over to touch me on the shoulder. I shrug away. I know I'm being unfair, but I can't help it. I know if she touches me, I'll start crying. And that's the last thing I want. "I'm your mother, Rayne. And I care about how you're feeling."

Yeah, right. She thinks she cares, but she isn't ready to hear the truth. That her precious daughter is a weirdo. A freak. A social reject with barely any friends and a father who doesn't even bother to show up to her birthday party.

If only that vampire thing had worked out to begin with. I could be miles away from this miserable existence. I could be living in the lavish underground coven with magic powers and riches beyond belief. My days could have been spent reading the classics. Studying philosophy to enrich my world. No schoolwork. No parents. Nothing but bliss.

Instead, I'm stuck here. In my mundane, horrible existence where no one understands me. Mom will never get it. She's too innocent to understand my depravity. She's too sweet to see the chaos that swirls under my skin. And I'm okay with that, actually. It's better that she live her life in her daisy-strewn optimism than know what a monster she created when she had me.

I think I must take after Dad.

"Rayne, I love you," Mom says, trying one more tactic. I know she'll give up soon and in a weird way this disappoints me.

"I know you do, Mom," I say resignedly.

Mom rises to her feet, her hazel eyes looking a bit watery. I feel terrible for putting her through this. For making her deal with me. Part of me wants to jump up and throw myself in her arms. Let her hold me and comfort me as I cry and tell her how much Dad hurt me by not showing up to my birthday. Take her strength since I have little left of my own.

But I can't find the willpower to get up from the bed. To lose face and admit weakness. So I sit scowling. More angry at myself than at her.

"If you ever want to talk, I'm here," she says. "I mean it."

"Thanks," I mumble, staring at my shoes, barely able to get the word out.

Mom pauses at the door. "I'm supposed to go out tonight, but . . . well, if you'd prefer I stay home, I will."

I look up. "Out?"

Mom's face gets red. "With David."

Great. She's still seeing David. Could my day get any worse?

"I don't think you should go out tonight . . . or ever," I mutter. "Not with him."

"Rayne, why? He's really nice. What do you have against him?" Mom lets out a frustrated breath. I can tell she's trying hard to be nice to me still, but at the same time she's ready to wring my neck. "Is it 'cause you feel he's going to replace your father?"

OMG! Does EVERYTHING in my freaking life have to revolve around Dad?

"Do you think I'm stupid?" I yell, scrambling to my feet, absolutely furious that she would even say such a thing. God, I wish that punching bag was here right about now. "Do you really think I'm holding out some kind of inane hope that the guy's gonna suddenly show up at our doorstep and want to be a family again? That's crazy, Mom! Really crazy!"

Mom takes a step backward, her eyes wide. I think she's afraid of me. Great. I've made my own mother afraid of me. I am a loser. Such a loser.

"Then what is it, Rayne? What's wrong with David?"

"There's nothing wrong with him. Nothing except for the fact that he's an evil vampire and I don't want him to kill you."

There. I said it. Let her deal with reality for once. I'm sick of sheltering her from the truth and looking like an idiot. Then again, in hindsight, telling one's mother that she's dating an evil vampire is probably not the best way to keep from looking idiotic.

Mom stares at me, her eyes narrowing and her lips pressed together tightly. She pauses for a moment and then speaks slowly and deliberately. "So you're trying to tell me that I shouldn't date David because he's a vampire."

"An evil vampire. If he was one of the good guys, I'd have no issue with it. In fact, I think it'd be kind of cool."

Realization lights on Mom's face. "Is that what you two were doing the other night with the garlic and the rosary beads?" she asks in a tight voice.

"Well, yes. Actually it was. It was a test. And he failed. Or passed—however you want to look at it. Bottom line, he *is* a vampire, Mom. And I don't think it's wise for you to be dating him because—"

"Rayne, this has gone far enough," Mom interrupts. "You obviously need help. I'm sending you back to Dr. Devlin. In fact, I'm going to see if he has any last-minute openings for tomorrow." She turns and storms out of the room, slamming the door behind her.

I slump back into my bed, tears of frustration springing to my eyes. Great. Just great. Now, in addition to Mom risking her life with Vamp Nerd, I'm going to be sent back to Dr. Devlin, psycho psychiatrist.

Let this be a lesson to all of you. No matter what happens, never tell your mom she's dating an evil vampire. It's just not worth it.

# 25

## I <3 Jareth and I Don't Care What U Think!

*Wow. So much has happened since I last wrote. Where to begin? I doubt I can write this as one big diary entry—it'd take me a week to type. I guess I can split it up into chapters. Not like anyone's reading this anymore. Sigh. I kind of miss my blog. It feels lonely writing to myself. . . .*

Luckily Dr. Devlin is booked up for about a month so I don't have to waste the evening talking to him about the symbolism of my dreams or whatever. After detention I go straight home and go straight to my room, yelling down that

I'm not interested in any dinner before slamming my door and blasting Snow Patrol from my stereo.

I turn off the light and lie on my bed, staring up at the ceiling. When Sunny and I were little we pasted glow-in-the-dark stars up there and there are still a few left, struggling to glow in their old age. It's kind of comforting to look at them. To remember a more innocent time.

I let my mind wander over the past week. The excitement of Dad coming. The disappointment of Dad not coming. The fight with Mike Stevens. The fight with Mom. The finding out that I have a destiny. The finding out that I have to share that destiny with a vampire who hates me. The realization that the vampire maybe isn't so bad.

I wonder where Jareth is. I haven't seen him since Wednesday night. He told me he'd call me when the results of the donor's blood came back from the lab, but it's already Tuesday and I haven't heard from him. Maybe he decided he'd be better off working alone. That he didn't need me.

The thought brings on the tears again. Jeez. I feel like I've cried more in the last three days than I have the rest of my life combined.

I'm such an idiot. To think Jareth might actually like me. That he might have been jealous when he saw me dancing with that other vamp. That he might have made up that excuse to kiss me in the broom closet just so he could do it. That there might be some kind of future with him.

Dumb, Rayne. Truly dumb.

Of course he doesn't want a future with me. What do I have to offer? Nothing. Absolutely nothing. My own father isn't interested in a future with me. Why should Jareth be?

Bleh.

I force myself to zone out to Snow Patrol, concentrating on the deep, melodious sounds and trying to block out the overwhelming sadness that's threatening to take me. A few minutes later I'm so into the music that I almost don't hear the knock on my door.

"Rayne?"

Mom. Great. I wonder if she's here to yell or to attempt comfort. I wonder which would be more annoying.

"Go away!" I cry, my voice sounding a bit wobbly. I hope she can't tell I've been crying. I don't want to give her the satisfaction.

"That's really nice, Rayne, thanks," she retorts. "And I'll be happy to. I just thought you might like to know there's a boy here to see you."

I raise my head and look over at the closed bedroom door. A boy? What boy would visit me? "Who is it?" I ask, against my better judgment.

"I've never seen him before," Mom says. "He says his name is Jareth. Tall, skinny. A bit on the pasty side? Dressed all in black, just how you like 'em," she adds, and I can hear a small smile in her voice. "Just hope he's not an evil vampire."

I wince a bit at the dig, but know she's doing her best to try to lighten things up between us. "Nah, he's not," I say with all the false bravado I can muster. "He's one of the good guys."

Mom laughs. "So I should send him up then?" she asks and I can hear the relief in her voice after what she thinks is my attempt at humor.

But no time for analyzing. Jareth is here. Here in my house. Soon to be here in my bedroom. Gah! I'm so unprepared. I glance around the room, realizing I have clothes strewn everywhere and that I'm wearing plaid flannel pants and a T-shirt.

"Rayne?"

"Uh, yeah, sure," I say, frantically grabbing discarded laundry and tossing it in the hamper. I'd normally ask if she could stall him for a moment or two, but I don't want her asking a thousand-year-old vampire about where he goes to high school.

I shed my clothes faster than Superman in a phone booth, tossing on a black-and-white plaid skirt and a Smiths concert T-shirt, then run over to the mirror.

Ugh. Even with the change of clothes I'm not looking so hot. My eyes are completely bloodshot from crying and my makeup's all smeared. I run my index finger under my eyes to try to get rid of the excess black. Then I apply more of my bloodred lipstick. Maybe that'll detract from the eyes.

A knock on the door causes my heart to jump in my throat. Why am I so nervous? It's just Jareth. We've been working together for nearly a week now. It's all business. And that one kiss? Well, it didn't mean anything. So there's absolutely no reason to freak.

Another knock. This one louder.

"Come in," I say, rushing back to my computer, as if I've been sitting there the whole time. No need for him to know he was worth reapplying lip gloss for.

He opens the door and steps over the threshold into my room. I've had guys in here before. Mom's cool with it as long as we keep the door open. But this seems different somehow. More dangerous. And since Jareth doesn't know the door rule, he shuts it behind him before walking over and sitting down on the bed. My bed. Gah! Jareth the hottest vampire ever is sitting on MY bed. I wish I had a web cam so I could have recorded the momentous event.

"So the blood test has come back from the lab," he says, launching right into business. "And it's positive."

Gulp. Good thing he shut the door. If Mom heard the words "blood test" and "positive" in the same sentence she'd be carting me away to the clinic before I could explain we were talking vampires, not HIV.

I turn around in my chair to face him. "Positive for . . . ?"

"Wait a moment." Jareth studies me with his intense blue eyes. "Have you been crying?"

I scowl. Great. I should have kept my back turned. "No. Of course not. I'm not your typical crying type of girl. Now, tell me about the donor's blood."

Jareth frowns. "Your eyes look red."

"Allergies."

"And your makeup's smudged."

"I dig the Mary-Kate Olsen look, what can I say?"

Jareth shakes his head. He's so not buying any of this. "What's wrong, Rayne? What happened?"

"Nothing."

"You're lying." He gets up from the bed and walks over to me, kneeling down in front of my chair, his earnest eyes searching my face. I turn my head to look back at the computer, mostly because his concerned expression has me this close to bursting into tears again.

"I'm not."

"Tell me what happened. Did someone hurt you?" He takes my hand in his and squeezes it lightly, his thumb caressing my palm. "You can tell me. It's okay."

And that, my friends, is the point that the dam breaks and the tears cascade down like Niagara Falls. How embarrassing. How pathetic. I can't believe I'm so weak. So vulnerable. He's going to think I'm the biggest loser on the planet. Maybe in the entire universe. If there was any chance he was at all interested in me, it's so gone now. I'm just another whiny, teary-faced human girl.

Jareth reaches up and swipes a tear away with his thumb. His touch is cool against my burning cheeks. "Tell me," he says in the most gentle voice you could imagine.

"Okay," I agree, realizing at this point I've got nothing to lose. I close my eyes resignedly and try to find my voice. I open my mouth to tell him the story of Mike Stevens, but something completely different comes out. Something I hadn't meant to share with anyone, let alone him.

"You know how I told you about my dad? How he left us four years ago to go 'find himself?' "

"Yes. Of course."

"Well, he's evidently still lost. I thought he was coming home for my birthday. Sunny and I turned seventeen three days ago and he sent us an e-mail saying he was going to come home to celebrate with us." I swallow hard. "It's so dumb, but . . ."

"But what?"

"I was so excited. My dad's awesome. Or he used to be anyway. And I haven't seen him in so long. I guess I thought maybe if he came . . . if he saw us again. Maybe he'd want to . . . I don't know . . ." I laugh bitterly. "Stick around or something. Or at least plan more regular visits. Sounds so stupid now that I think about it."

Jareth shakes his head. "Not stupid at all," he says. "It makes perfect sense to me."

"Anyway, it doesn't matter. He never showed. He was

supposed to bring the cake, too." I laugh bitterly. "We ended up having a birthday party with no cake. Pretty lame, huh?"

"Did he call to tell you why? Did something happen to prevent him from making it?"

"No. I waited up 'til like one A.M., hoping he'd walk through the door. So idiotic." My voice breaks again and I'm sobbing like crazy now. Can we say LOSER? "Sunny e-mailed him the next day. Turns out some other thing came up and he says he forgot to tell us."

"Other thing?"

"Evidently he's got a new wife. And she has kids. One of them had some school play or something . . ." I shrug. "Why go hang with the old family, I guess, when you've got a whole new one?"

Without warning, Jareth grabs me and pulls me into a hug. At first I'm not sure about this, but his arms feel so right, wrapped around me. His hands so good, stroking my back. I give in, burying my head in his shoulder and sobbing my eyes out. Trying to take the strength he is offering me. I'm scared to death at the perfect comfort I receive, but too relieved to pull away.

"I'm so sorry, Raynie," he whispers, smoothing my hair with his hands. "That's a lousy thing to do. He doesn't deserve you as a daughter."

"I wish I could just hate him," I cry, hoping my nose isn't all running on Jareth's black shirt. "But I can't. I still love him. I still miss him. No matter what he does, he's still my dad."

"It's hard when people you love let you down."

"Sometimes I think that's why I don't have any close friends," I say, now in full-on babble mode. I can't believe I'm telling him all this. But his arms feel warm and his touch is comforting. I haven't felt so safe in eons. "I mean, everyone thinks it's 'cause I'm some tough punk-rock chick who doesn't need anyone. But, in reality, I think it's 'cause I'm scared to death. That if I get close to someone, they'll just leave."

"I know the feeling," Jareth says, almost thoughtfully. "More than you can know."

"Oh?" Excitement builds inside me, competing with my sadness. He's on the verge of spilling the Deep Dark Secret, I can tell.

He pulls his head away. "Some other time," he says, pressing his lips against my forehead and giving me a soft kiss.

I stick out my lower lip in a mock pout. "Oh, fine."

He laughs. "I promise."

"I'll hold you to that."

"Don't worry," he says, reaching over to my nightstand and grabbing me a tissue. He hands it to me and I wipe my eyes and nose. "Unlike some people, I keep my promises. Always and forever."

He reaches up and brushes a strand of hair out of my eyes

and studies my face. "You're really beautiful," he says. "You know that?"

I screw up my face. "Yeah, yeah." But secretly I'm pleased.

"No. I'm serious." His fingers trail down the side of my face, his nails lightly scraping at my cheekbone. Feels so good. I close my eyes.

And then he kisses me. Yes, the beautiful vampire, the dark general, the one who never gets close to anyone, leans in and presses his lips against mine.

This kiss is different than the one in the closet. This kiss is soft. Gentle. Light. Like a butterfly's wing whisking my lips. I know it sounds weird, but it's almost like a worshipful caress. I sigh a bit as tingly sensations burst from my fingers, my toes—all over my body. I kiss him back, hesitantly at first and then with more assurance. Jareth is a master kisser, nothing like the awkward fumbling boys I've dated in the past. The ones more interested in the technical workings of my bra. The ones who see the mouth only as an obligatory precursor to getting me to take off my clothes. But Jareth seems content just to kiss me. To explore my mouth with his own. His tongue telling a thousand stories, mine delighting in a thousand tastes.

I wonder what he's thinking as he kisses me. Does he have feelings for me? Is this something he's been hoping will happen? Or is this just a gesture meant to cheer me up, to distract me from my pain? Sadly, I have no real clue what this immortal creature of the night actually feels for me and that scares me to death.

*Stop thinking so much,* Rayne, I tell myself. *You've got a hot guy making out with you in your bedroom. Just go with it.*

But I can't. Not this time. Because I'm starting to develop a deep tenderness for this vampire. And that's pretty damn terrifying. After all, he's told me a dozen times that he doesn't get close to anyone. He doesn't even have donors, for goodness sake. He never wants a blood mate. He likes being alone. If I fall for him, I'm going to fall alone. And when I hit rock bottom, it's going to hurt like crazy. In fact, I'm not sure I'd even be able to survive. To claw my way up from such heartbreak.

And so, as much as it sucks, I force myself to pull away. He stares at me dully for a moment, as if in a daze, then frowns. "What's wrong?" he asks in a wounded voice that breaks my heart.

"Nothing," I say briskly, scrambling to my feet. I cross my arms over my chest. "So let's get back to business."

"But—" The hurt on his face is unmistakable and I feel like a monster. Still, even though he's a vampire, he's also a guy. And guys can get like that after they've been denied sex. In fact, I'd be willing to bet he doesn't care one lick about me as a person. He just wants to jump me. Just like everyone else. And I'm so not interested.

"You said you got the blood test results back. What did you learn?"

He sighs deeply and then rises to his feet, running a hand through his dirty blond hair. He stares into the mirror. Unlike in the movies and TV shows, vamps DO have reflections and his, I notice, is not one of a happy vampire. But that can't be helped, I guess.

I feel bad, but I tell myself that in the long run, it's better this way. After all, this can't go anywhere. It can't become anything. So just rip off the Band-Aid and move on to the next scene.

"Well, that's the strange thing," he says at last, evidently resigning himself to the fact that he's not getting any more nookie from this chick. "It's definitely contaminated with some kind of blood-borne virus, but we're not exactly sure what. Whatever it is, our scientists believe it's the same virus that's affected Kristoff. Obviously vampires don't die like humans, but somehow the virus has been able to weaken him and take away his powers."

"How is Kristoff, anyway?"

"About the same. Not sick. Not exactly. Just weak. And powerless. It's the strangest thing."

"Poor guy."

"Indeed. And he's not the only one. Several of the coven's top leaders have come down with a very similar illness. And all their donors are dead."

"Wow. That's terrible. So do you think it's being spread through the donors? Remember, we saw Kristoff's donors at the Blood Bar. Could it be possible that Maverick is behind this?"

"I do. In fact, I'd say it's quite probable," Jareth says, nodding. "It's my theory that this is the way Maverick hopes to overthrow Magnus's rule. By crippling Magnus's strong supporters, he can weaken his command, and then stage a coup."

"Actually, that's exactly what the Slayer Inc. guy, Teifert, says," I tell him. "He suggested we go back to the Blood Bar and see if we can find a sample of the original virus itself. Maybe they have a room where they store it all. Maybe they even have some kind of antidote there." I jump up from my seat, eager to be out of these closed quarters, lest I do something stupid like jump his vampire bones again. "We should go now. Time is a-wasting."

Jareth shakes his head. "I should go now. Not we. You will stay home."

"What? No way! I'm so not staying home."

"This could be dangerous."

"But I'm Raynie the Vampire Slayer," I say, grabbing the stake off my computer table and raising it in the air.

Jareth chuckles. "Oh, yes. I forgot. Very scary."

"Come on," I whine. "Please? It's, like, my destiny and stuff, remember? Just let me come. I need an adventure. I can't keep sitting around moping in my room."

"Okay, fine. But you have to listen to me. Do as I say. No

heroics here," he insists. "You may have a stake, but I'd bet my fangs you don't know how to use it."

"Not true. I got some Slayer Training this weekend. I'm now the stake mastah!"

"Ah. Impressive." Jareth smiles. "Can't wait to see you in action."

"So should we head over now?"

"Hm." Jareth looks at his watch. "Actually it's only eight. The Blood Bar will be open 'til two A.M. and we want to hit them closer to closing time."

"Oh, okay." A bit disappointed, I set the stake back down on the desk. So much for immediate distraction. "Uh, I guess just come pick me up when you're ready to leave?" Hopefully by then Mom will be in bed. I doubt she'd be cool with me leaving the house at one thirty on a school night.

"Actually, I was wondering if you'd like to . . . do something with me first," Jareth says, sounding a bit shy all of a sudden.

I look up, surprised. "Uh, what?"

"Go dancing."

"Dancing? Now?" Wow. That is so not what I expected him to say. Though I don't know what I did expect. A shiver of delight makes its way up my backbone. Dancing. With Jareth. Mmm.

Jareth shrugs. "Yes. Why not?"

Bleh. I know I should say no. Keep ripping off the Band-Aid.

Not put myself in a position where the two of us could easily hook up. Dancing is powerful and dangerous and if I want to stay at arm's length it's the last thing I should agree to.

"I don't know. No reason, I guess. It's just—" *Just that I'm not strong enough not to melt when you take me into your arms.*

"Remember what we talked about at Club Fang the other night? About losing oneself in the music? Seeking peace inside the dance?" He smiles at me. "I think someone's in need of a little of that right about now."

Oh. So that's what he means. An unwarranted disappointment floats through me. Bleh. I should have known. He has no secret agenda to hook up with me. This is just a simple cheer-up technique to get my mind back on the job. Well, that's better, I suppose. Safer, at least. And something I can justify doing.

He's still looking at me expectantly and I realize that I haven't given him a verbal answer. "I'd love to," I reply.

He takes my hand and pulls me to my feet, then ushers me to my bedroom door, hand brushing against the small of my back. Gah. His touch really should be illegal. Almost makes me want to skip the dance club and go straight for the bed. Not that that would be a good idea. And besides, I kind of like this almost old-fashioned chivalrous thing he's got going on. So unlike guys my age, who are just interested in getting it on with the Goth freak.

Besides, we've already established that he's just being nice. He probably feels sorry for me and my pathetic little lost-daddy's-girl thing. Ugh.

We tell Mom we're going out and she looks so pleased that I've actually left my bedroom I bet if I told her we were off to smoke crack and get lap dances she would have waved and said, "Have a good time. Just be back by curfew."

We jump in Jareth's BMW and speed off to Club Fang. He turns the music up extra loud, just the way I like it, and I zone out to the crooning sounds of Morrissey. It's nice and comfortable this way. No awkward convo and strained silences. He must sense that I've already shared way more than I ever share and am currently all talked out.

Club Fang is hopping when we get there. After paying the bouncer the cover charge, we walk inside and are enveloped by darkness, illuminated only by irregular flashing strobe lights and obscured by machine-created fog. The bass is up, the music is dark and enchanting, and I'm in Heaven already.

Jareth grabs my hand and together we weave through the crowd of sweaty gothed-out dancers until we get to the center of the room. Then he pulls me close and together we start swaying to the music.

At first I'm thinking, "Danger, danger!" and that I should not be here. With him. Falling deeper and deeper for a guy who doesn't want me for anything more than friendship. But as the music takes me, my reservations start melting away. I'm here. I'm in his arms. I might as well accept things. Take them for what they are and enjoy the moment. Who knows when something so blissful will come around again.

As we dance, my troubles seem more and more trivial. I mean, so what if my dad didn't show up for my birthday? It's not like he's a regular at any other family events. We've been fine without him for the last four years and we'll be fine without him for the next four. And so what if Mike Stevens is a huge dick with an attitude? High school will be the best years of his life. Soon he'll be strapped with five kids, a job that gives him ulcers, and a wife who doesn't understand him.

None of it matters in the long run. Just the beat. The tribal sounds that stir something primitive inside of me. At this very moment there is no past. No future. Just a vampire's arms wrapped around me, his hot body pressed against mine. Heaven.

Jareth seems lost in it, too. His eyes are closed as he sways against me. I study his face as the multicolored lights dance across it, creating alternating shadows and light. I wonder again what he's hiding. What turmoil and hurt lies under his calm exterior. What has made him so angry? What has made him so like me?

Because he is like me, I realize. He hides his torment, conceals his pain, until he can't anymore and then it explodes and he comes across as a nasty, angry person. But he's not really like that. Not inside.

The beat slows and so does our dance. Jareth's eyes open, almond-shaped sapphires that practically glow in the dark. I know I keep harping on them, but I've just never seen such beautiful eyes before and I'm sure I never will again. He reaches down and brushes a lock of hair away from my sweaty forehead.

"How are you?" he asks. And the way he says it makes me believe that he actually cares about the answer.

"Better," I say, smiling up at him. "Much better, actually."

"Sometimes it's good to talk," he says. "But other times you'd rather just lose your mind."

I nod, amazed at how his thoughts totally parallel mine. He really is the perfect guy in so many ways.

Screw it. I might as well face the facts: I'm in love. And there's nothing I can do about it.

# 26

We park down the street from the Blood Bar and go inside separately. Jareth goes through the employee entrance and I go through the front door.

"Hey, Shaniqua," Francis greets, smiling at me as I approach. "Thought I'd finally seen the last of you."

"Can't scare me away that easily, Frannie," I shoot back with a grin of my own.

"Luckily for me or I'd miss out on all this witty banter."

"Didn't I tell you that I'd grow on you? You should always listen to me. Always."

"Hey. I do. Heck, if you told me to jump, girl, I'd only have to ask how high."

We laugh for moment. Then I turn to more serious business. "So," I lower my voice, "did you find your blood mate?"

His smile dips into a frown. "Yes," he says, shoving his hands in his jean pockets. "It's the weirdest thing. She's evidently been inflicted with some sort of horrible virus. I mean, she's really sick. She can barely sit up. And worst of all, I think she's lost all her vampiric powers. Of course, she's convinced herself that once she's better she'll get them back, but honestly I'm not so sure."

Wow. Another vampire with ties to the Blood Bar who has come down with the virus. There's definitely something rotten in Denmark.

"No one seems to know what's wrong with her. The scary part is, she's not the only sick one. A lot of her fellow biters have been coming down with it. One day they're at work, sucking away like nothing's wrong, the next they're gone, replaced by some vampire we've never seen before. I've tracked a few of the missing vamps down and everyone seems to have contracted the same sickness."

"Have you talked to management?"

"We've tried, but they've refused to speak with our union reps. They say nothing's wrong and that they don't want us to panic the others with our 'delusions.'" Francis rubs his bald head with the back of his hand. "Honestly, I don't know what to do at this point."

I'm not quite sure what to do myself. This is all becoming far too clear, but I'm not sure who I should trust. Would Francis help me? After all, his blood mate has been affected, and he seems to love her an awful lot. But would he go against his employer? Risk his job and life? And what if he doesn't believe me? What if he grabs his Nextel and calls Maverick to report me? I might be able to get away, but Jareth is still inside.

At least I'm beginning to understand what's going on. The biters are evidently given the virus, unaware. Then, they unwittingly pass it off to the donors, who in turn pass it to their employers. The real targets are obviously the higher-up vampires in Magnus's circle. Like Kristoff. People who keep things running at the coven. We're extremely lucky, I realize, that Jareth gets his blood by mail order and doesn't keep donors himself. Otherwise, I'm sure he'd have been targeted as well.

I make my decision, deciding to trust Francis. After all, he's been personally affected by this dastardly plot. And the people getting sick are his friends and coworkers.

"Okay, Frannie, listen up. Here's the deal. In reality, I'm not your typical Blood Bar patron. I've actually been sent here, undercover." I stop before mentioning who actually sent me. The idea that I'm the Vampire Slayer should probably be left as a need-to-know.

His eyes widen. "Undercover?"

"You know the Blood Coven, formerly run by Lucifent and now run by Magnus?"

"Of course," Francis says. "Everyone knows about the coven. My blood mate has been on a waiting list to join for years. I tried to tell her that they don't take people like us, but she never gives up hope."

Ugh. Vampire segregation? Is Magnus's coven actually an elitist op? I so need to talk to him about that when this is all done. That's so not cool that he leaves people out.

"Our boss, Maverick, the guy who owns the Blood Bar, is a member," Francis adds. "In fact, from what he says, I take it he's next in line for the throne or something." The vampire snorts. "The guy's such an arrogant jerk. Who knows if that's true or not."

"Francis, listen to me carefully," I interject. "Magnus, Master of the Blood Coven, believes that Maverick may be staging a takeover. He wants to be in charge. And since he doesn't have enough vamp power to start an outright war, instead we believe he's created some kind of virus. The virus is injected into the high-ranking coven members' donors and then the donors pass it along to their vampires. All of Magnus's loyal subjects become sick and weak. Maybe even Magnus himself. Then Maverick moves in and takes over."

Francis stares at me. "That seems a bit complicated."

"But don't you see? It could totally work. Is already working, actually. Your friends aren't the only ones who are sick. Several coven bigwigs have also come down with the disease."

"But why are my coworkers being infected? They're not even members of the Blood Coven."

"They're the innocents, being used by Maverick to advance his personal gain," I say. "He probably injects them somehow so they'll pass the disease off to the donors." I bite my lower lip, thinking. "But how do they infect the biters, I wonder. Has anything been different lately, Francis?"

He shrugs. "I don't think so."

"Think harder. Some change in routine? Some new policy or procedure?"

I can see the idea lightbulb flash over his head. "The vitamin injections," he murmers.

"What?"

"A few weeks ago some of the biters, including Dana, were told they were going to start getting weekly vitamin shots. To keep healthy. We thought it was a bit strange. After all, vampires don't usually get sick." Francis squeezes his large hands into fists. "That bastard!" he growls. "He infected her! Why, I should go down there and just kill him. Right here, right now."

I shake my head. "Bad idea, Frannie. You'd just get overpowered by the others. And we don't know who we can trust at this point. Some of the employees must be in on this, or else it couldn't be running so smoothly."

"Right. Of course, you're right." He sighs. "So what can we do? I want to help in any way I can."

"Okay, good," I say, relieved to have him on board. "I have a vampire working with me who's been posing as an employee. He's already inside," I explain. "Can you help us get down into the restricted areas of the Blood Bar? We need to find out where they're keeping the virus so we can bring a sample back to our labs for analysis. Our scientists believe if they have a vial of the stuff, they may be able to create an antidote."

"And if your coven creates the antidote, will you share it with us?" Francis asks. "Those of us who aren't members?"

"Of course," I say, hoping that's true. Well, I'll make sure it is. No vamp discrimination in my book. "There will be enough vaccine for anyone who needs it."

"You're a good person, you know that?" Francis asks. "I'm glad I let you in that first day."

"As if you could resist me." I grin. "Now tell me what you think we should do."

# 27

## The Not-So-Great Virus Heist

Francis proves to be the best hookup ever. I doubt we could have done any of this without him. First, he sends me inside and I request Jareth as my biter. Once Jareth and I are together in our room, we wait. Francis shows up a moment later, costumes in hand.

"Maverick actually owns this whole block," he explains. "And so there's a huge sprawling basement under this building. Most of the areas are restricted, but I always see the employees who work down there dressed in these." He holds out the clothes. White scrubs, complete with surgical masks.

"Cool. Where did you get them?" I ask.

He laughs. "I, uh, borrowed them from some employees I

thought needed a little nap. So you'd better do this quick, before they wake up and figure out how to get themselves untied and out of the linen closet."

"Wow, very nice, Frannie." I hold up one of the outfits. "Now we'll fit right in. Thanks so much."

"Anything to help Dana," he says with a sheepish shrug. But I can tell he's pleased by the compliment. "Let me know if I can do something else."

"No. This is great," Jareth says, slipping the shirt over his head. "You'd better get back to the door before anyone becomes suspicious. Rayne and I can take it from here."

"Okay," he says. "The stairs to the basement are at the far end of the hallway. The employees were nice enough to leave their keycards in the pockets of those uniforms." He grins. "Good luck."

He exits the room and we scramble to don our scrubs and masks. Once outfitted, we nod to one another. This is it.

We find the staircase easily and swipe our keycards, then head downstairs. Francis wasn't kidding. The underground is huge, full of windy corridors and closed doors. The dim fluorescent lighting and low ceilings don't make it any more comforting either.

We try a few doors with our keycards, and at first none seem to work. But there are so many doors, I guess it'll take a while to find the right one. Hopefully no one will catch us randomly trying locks. Might seem a bit suspicious.

But luck is with us. Jareth points at an employee dressed just like us, exiting a door at the far end of the corridor. I nod. Together, we casually walk down the hall, keeping our steps at a normal pace, until we reach the door.

This time, the keycards work and the door swings silently open.

We step into the room and my mouth drops open in shock. The place is like a regular laboratory, with Bunsen burners burning, test tubes bubbling, the works. Whatever Maverick's got planned, it's a full-scale operation. He's got a couple employee vamps in the back, dressed as we are with face masks and scrubs, mixing some kind of multicolored powders together. They turn and acknowledge us, then turn back to their work. Phew. The disguises work. Thank you, Francis.

Jareth beckons me over to the left wall, taken up by the hugest refrigerators I've ever seen. He wraps his hand around the door handle and pulls one open. Puffy white freezer smoke billows out.

Inside there are rows upon rows upon rows upon rows of tiny medicine bottles. Like the kind you stick syringes into. Each bottle is labeled with an "M" which I suppose is for Maverick. Or maybe Murder and Mayhem. Or heck, it could stand for Mickey Mouse for all I know. But what was I expecting? A vial with a warning label? *Do not consume this product if you are a vampire or a human who lets vampires snack on them.*

"Let's take two of the vials," Jareth suggests in a low voice. "We'll bring them back to our lab for testing. To see if they match up with what the donors were infected with."

I nod and reach for one of the vials.

"Wait!" Jareth warns, but he's too late. The room suddenly explodes with sirens and multicolored flashing lights.

Uh, oh. Not good.

"Damn it!" Jareth cries. "You must have tripped some alarm." He glances anxiously around the room. The two employees in the back are staring at us. I can't see their expressions under the masks, but I'm thinking the looks aren't of friendly disinterest anymore.

"What do we do?" I hiss, my heart pounding like crazy in my chest. They didn't cover this in Slayer 101.

Jareth pushes me forward. "Run!" he cries. "And don't stop until you're free and clear of this place." He grabs two vials and pushes them into my hand. "Bring these directly to Magnus. Do not stop, whatever you do."

"But what about you?" I cry, realizing he's planning on going all heroic on me and not being sure I want him to. What if he gets hurt? Captured? Killed, even?

Jareth glances over at the two employees, who are making long strides in our direction.

"I'll distract them. Head them off. Hurry!"

"But what if they—"

"For hell's sake, Rayne, for once in your life just do something without arguing!"

And so I do. I dash down the corridor, weaving through the maze of passages, trying to remember which one leads to the stairs. All around me the lights are still flashing, the sirens still wailing. I hope Jareth is okay. What will they do to him if they catch him? What if they inject him with the virus? What if he gets sick? It'll all be my fault for setting off the alarm.

Suddenly I slam face first into a solid wall. A solid wall of flesh, to be more precise. I look up, swallowing hard as my eyes focus on the man standing in front of me. I'd recognize that face anywhere. Those hypnotic, icy eyes. That cruel stare.

Maverick.

"Uh, I'm, well, I work, uh, lost . . ." Panic has effectively robbed me of coherent sentence-forming abilities. Not that for one moment I think even if I could suddenly speak as eloquently as Bono I'd have any better chance of escaping with my life.

Because I'm caught. By the big baddie himself.

But wait! I'm the Vampire Slayer. I can kill him, right? I reach behind me and whip out my stake. The normally dull piece of wood suddenly erupts in a fiery light as I wave it into the air, just like what happened in the gym at school. w00t!

"Don't come any closer," I say in my most menacing tone, wielding the stake like a sword, ready to swing and stab.

*Yeah, baby! Who's scary now!?*

# 28

## Maverick Is a Meanie

Sadly, my victory dance is short-lived. Mainly because Maverick refuses to look all scared and worried at the sight of the glowy stake. Even more so when he starts laughing instead of shaking in his boots. Damn it, what does a slayer chick have to do to get a little respect around here?

"Um, you know, I'll kill you," I add, in case he doesn't get the message. Maybe he doesn't understand. When I show up, he should run. "I'm Raynie the Vampire Slayer."

This time, to my utter annoyance, his laughter goes from a small chuckle to a big rolling belly laugh. He raises his arm and suddenly the stake goes flying out of my hand and right into his. He catches it with ease and it stops doing the glowy thing and becomes just another piece of half-carved wood. He tosses it over his shoulder and it clatters to the ground behind him.

Great. Well, so much for that idea. Now what?

They say when you're in this kind of situation, your body gears up for one of two things: fight or flight. Well, without my magical stick, I figure I'll be a pretty pathetic fighter, so I choose option B and turn tail.

Unfortunately, Maverick must have summoned some additional Vin Diesel–looking guards while I was waving my useless stake around and so when I turn, I turn right into them. They grab me and drag me, kicking and screaming, down the hallway and into a small, windowless room, complete with cobwebs and shackles. It screams medieval dungeon and you goths would love it. Heck, I would have loved it, if I was not pretty convinced that the room was to be my death chamber.

I wonder if Jareth got out. Maybe he did. Maybe he can get help from the coven.

Maverick watches as his men push me into a wooden chair and then chain me to the wall. They're not gentle and the shackles pinch my wrists. Not that I'm much worried about bruising at this point. As long as my heart's still beating, I'm ahead of the game.

"You'll never get away with this," I shout, mainly because that's what you always hear people shouting in the movies when they're in an impossible situation like this. In the back of my mind, of course, I realize that more than likely he *is* going to get away with this. With all of this. In real life the bad guys do live happily ever after. If you don't believe me, take a look at my dad.

"And what, pray tell, do you think I will not get away with?" Maverick asks, folding his thin arms across his chest. He's wearing black leather pants, a vinyl fetish vest, and a velvet cape. A total *Glamour* "don't," let me tell you.

"Poisoning Magnus's people with your stupid blood-borne virus," I say. "We're totally on to you and know what you're doing. And we're going to stop you. Maybe not me specifically, but I am one of many."

"I see," Maverick says, stroking his goatee with his index finger and thumb. "Do you, by chance, know Rachel and Charity?"

At first I have no idea who he's talking about, then something reminds me. "Magnus's donors?" Fear grips my heart as I wait for what he's going to say next.

Maverick smiles a stereotypical evil villain smile. "Yes. Magnus's donors. Charming girls. We had them as our guests tonight at the Blood Bar."

"Why would they come to the Blood Bar?" I ask, trying to puzzle out the last piece. How come all these donors, who already get bitten on a daily basis, are coming to the bar of their own free will? Why would they need to get sucked?

"Easy. Because they're stupid vampire wannabes, the lot of them," Magnus explains. "We forged some blood mate invitations from the coven. They think they're coming here to finally achieve their lifelong dream. To become vampires."

Ah. Pretty clever, though, of course, maniacally evil.

"And you poison them instead. And then send them back to poison their own vampires. You evil bastard."

"You shouldn't keep dishing out these delectable compliments, my dear," Maverick says with a grin. "But, yes, the donors, including Rachel and Charity tonight, have all been poisoned. And as soon as Magnus indulges in his nightly meal, he will be poisoned, too. In a few days he will lose all his powers and thus be unable to run the coven."

"But why? What do you have against Magnus?"

Maverick shrugs. "Nothing, really. Except he's got my job."

"That's BS. It's his job. He's Lucifent's first sire."

"Sure, that's the nonsense he goes around spouting," Maverick says, squeezing his black fingernailed hands into fists. "But it's not true. I was Lucifent's first. But he disowned me back in the nineteenth century because of a minor unpleasantness."

I can't even begin to imagine what unpleasantness he's talking about, or just how minor it really was. But now I do get why Maverick is so out for Magnus.

"So if you're all hell-bent on revenge, why not just go

attack Magnus personally? This blood virus thing is a bit on the overly elaborate side, don't you think?"

"I had to create something that would weaken all of Magnus's forces, not just him. If I just killed him, some other annoying leader would step into his place. Like that weepy little moron Jareth or something."

Jareth. Even the name conjures up a small amount of hope inside of me. If he'd made it out alive he could go get help. Get the army to come and rescue me. I could live to fail at slaying another day.

"This way I will have slowly destroyed all his followers from within, before any of those idiots know what hit them. The Blood Coven will be in code red and I'll step in to guide them to a better future."

"And then I'll slay you," I say, trying to keep up the brave front.

He shakes his head. "No. You won't, because you will be dead."

Before I'm quite sure what's happening, he's on me, having crossed the room in a nanosecond, so fast my eyes can't follow. He's close, pressing his body against mine, his sour breath making me turn up my nose. (Maybe the movie WAS right about horrid breath being a sign of a vamp.) He pushes my head to the side, exposing my neck, and leans in, his fangs digging into my sensitive skin.

I cry in anguish as the pain shoots like lightning through

my veins, burning with unquenchable fire. It's like nothing I've ever felt. I grit my teeth and try desperately to remember Jareth's bite—the sweetness, the ecstasy—but all I can feel now is the scorching heat, like it's boiling my blood. I swallow hard, trying with all my might not to cry. I don't want him to see that he has won. Even though I'm pretty sure he already knows.

At least it doesn't last long. He wrenches his fangs out of me and I can feel warm blood seeping down my neck. It's gushing out and my hands are tied, so I can't put any pressure on it to stop it. For a moment, I wonder if I'll bleed to death.

Maverick licks his crimson-stained lips. "I've always wondered what a slayer tastes like. A lot sweeter than I expected." He pulls a vial out of his pocket and screws off the eyedropper cap. Squeezing a small amount of the vial's liquid into the dropper, he walks back over to me.

When I realize what he's about to do, I try to struggle, make my neck as difficult to reach as possible. But being chained, I don't have much leeway. He manages to empty the contents of the dropper into my gaping neck wound.

"There," he says, stepping back. "That wasn't so hard, now, was it?"

"What did you do?" I ask through gritted teeth.

"Hm, for a slayer you're not all that bright," he comments. "You've been infected with the virus, of course. In three days, you will die." He pats me on the shoulder. "And no, there is no magical antidote like you always see in the movies."

I'm suddenly cold, my heart slamming against my rib cage as reality sinks in. Oh, my god. I'm going to die. In three days, I'll be dead. I'll never make it to eighteen. I'll never graduate from high school. I'll never see my mother or sister or Spider again. I'll never see Jareth again.

"But don't worry, love," Maverick says. "I'm not going to keep you chained here for your last days. You'll be free to go." He motions to the two guards standing at the door's entrance. "Guards, release her," he says. "And escort her out."

Well, that was something, at least. I guess. I could say my good-byes. Hug my mother and sister one more time. I wonder if my dying days would be enough motivation for Dad to come by for a visit. I suppose if it didn't conflict with Bratty Stepchild #2's baseball schedule, I might have a chance.

Tears threaten to fall again and I bite down hard on my lower lip to stop it from quivering. I must stay strong. Let him think I'm fearless. Don't give him the power of seeing me weak.

The guards unlock my arms from their shackles and I gratefully get up from the chair. Maverick is still grinning maniacally at me, so very pleased with himself.

"They will crown me Master of the Coven," he crows. "When they learn I was the one who took down the slayer."

I stare at him, suddenly realizing exactly what I have to

do. He's underestimating me. Underestimating who I am. I'm not just any old sniveling girl who will go quietly into the night to lick my wounds. I am the Slayer. The one chosen once in a generation to kill evil vampires.

I have a destiny. And it's time to fulfill it.

I close my eyes for a moment, searching for the strength I need. Concentrating, as Teifert told me I could. Trying to be Zen and all that.

And then I find it. Something lying dormant, deep inside of me. Almost like a big ball of light, straining against its chains, dying to be released. I squeeze my eyes and channel that light with all that I have inside me and suddenly I explode with energy and power.

I open my eyes. I am the slayer. Here me roar.

A quick roundhouse kick takes out one of the guards. The other I head butt and then kick in the groin as he's reeling backward. I'm punching and kicking so hard, so fast, I'm not quite sure where my body ends and my target begins. It's like I'm on some kind of superhero autopilot.

And let me tell you, it rocks!

Having knocked out both guards I turn to Maverick. He's standing there, backed up against the wall, looking a lot less smug than before. "You can't kill me," he says, sounding a bit hoarse. "You don't have your stake."

"Stake, schmake," I say, suddenly realizing something. "You ever see the movie *Dumbo*?"

He stares at me as if I have two heads. "*Dumbo*?" he asks.

I laugh, suddenly feeling in complete control of the situation. "Yeah," I say. "Dumbo's a flying elephant. But the thing about Dumbo is, he only thinks he can fly because he's got some stupid magic feather in his trunk. But turns out," I say, circling Maverick, hands raised in front of me, "he doesn't need the feather at all. He can fly all along."

"As charming as this Disney fairy tale is—"

"But don't you see, Maverick?" I interrupt. "I'm Dumbo. Well, except for the big ears. And the actual flying bit. Okay, maybe bad analogy. But the point is, I don't need some special stake to slay you. The power is in *me*, not some chunk of wood."

And before Maverick can reply, I fluidly grab the chair, break off its leg and slam the piece of wood into his evil heart. He explodes instantly into a pile of dust.

Whoo-hoo! I am the SLAY-ERRR BAY-BEE!!!!!!!

I contemplate slaying the unconscious guards as well, but realize they may just be evil for the paycheck and now that their fearless leader has gone all "ashes to ashes" they may re-form and become model vampire citizens. You never know.

The important thing is I did the job. I slayed Maverick. Fulfilled my destiny. Saved the day.

Yay, me!

But then my exultation dampens as I remember that while I may have saved the Blood Coven, I failed to save myself. I drop the stake and fall to my knees, sobbing uncontrollably.

I'm going to die. In three days I will no longer exist.

That totally bites.

# 29

## Fangs for the Memories

"Rayne! Are you okay?"

I look up, trying to focus through my tears. Jareth and another man rush into the room. Jareth throws his arms around me and squeezes me so hard I practically lose my breath.

"Rayne," he murmurs. "You're all right, you're okay. I was so worried!" He strokes my hair and kisses me softly on the cheek. "I got backup. I was coming to save you."

"Silly vampire," I say, laughing through my tears. "I'm the slayer, remember? I can save myself. Well, sort of. But we can talk about that later." Now is not the time to tell him about my swiftly approaching expiration date. We've still got too much to do.

I can feel his smile against my cheek. If only he knew. "Right. Of course. So you finally figured out how to wield your magical stake?"

"Actually, I finally learned that the stake didn't have any magic. When it comes to vamps, any old piece of wood will do."

Jareth pulls away, looking at my bleeding neck. I'm sure it's nice and crusty-looking by now. "You've been bitten!" he cries, reaching out to touch the wound. I stop him before he does. The last thing I need is for him to get infected, too.

"It's okay," I lie. "It doesn't hurt."

"You have done well, Rayne," the man who entered with Jareth says. I look up in surprise. I forgot he was here. "Teifert will be pleased."

My eyes widen as I recognize the guy.

David?

Mom's boyfriend?

"You're . . . but you're . . ."

David laughs. "Yes, it's me, Rayne."

"But how . . . ? Who . . . ?"

"I work for Slayer Inc.," he explains. He pulls out an official-looking Slayer Inc. badge to back up his claim. "As your guardian."

"Guardian? I have a guardian?"

"What, did you think we'd leave you floundering out in the world alone on your first slay?"

"But why didn't you tell me? I thought you were a vampire!"

David laughs. "Is that why you tried to feed me garlic and squirt me with holy water when I came to dinner?"

Jareth raises an eyebrow. "You did what?"

I can feel my face getting *sooo* red. "Well, I didn't know he was my freaking guardian. I thought he was just some evil vampire Mom picked up in the frozen foods section."

David shuffles his feet. "About that, Rayne," he says. "I have to admit, I was told to get close to your family. To watch you and see how you do. Your first slay is a test. So we observe carefully. Anyway, I figured dating your mom would get me into your house, so I could get a better idea of your home life."

"That's a rotten thing to do," I interrupt, not at all happy about this. He may not be a vamp, but I'll find some other way to dust him if he's been screwing around with my mom's head just to get close to me. "My mom really likes you. And you're just using her?"

"Hey! Wait a minute!" David holds up his hands. "Hear me out. As I said, that's how it started. But then I actually met your mother. And she's . . . wonderful."

"I already know that she's wonderful. She's my mom." I scowl.

David sighs. "Look. What I'm trying to say is I like your mom very much. And now that the assignment is over I'd like to be allowed to continue dating her. If that's okay with you."

I scrunch up my eyes, still not quite sure. "Well, we'll see," I say. "Maybe. If she still wants you."

"Thanks," he says. "I'll take what I can get. Don't worry," he adds, "I'll prove to you that I'm a worthy suitor."

His words bring me back to reality and the fact that I won't get to see how this relationship plays out. Because I'll be dead. Long dead and buried, with worms crawling out of my eye sockets.

I turn back to Jareth. He's staring at me with such concern. I wish the two of us could be alone. I've got to tell him about my impending doom. Let him hold me as I cry in his arms.

Then I remember. "Magnus!" I cry. "We've got to warn Magnus!"

"Warn him?"

"Rachel and Charity are infected! If he drinks their blood he's going to lose his powers, just like the others."

Jareth pulls out his cell phone and dials Magnus's number. After a moment's pause he greets his boss and tells him what happened, warning him not to drink from his donors.

He clicks off the phone after saying good-bye. "I reached him in time," he says. "Rachel and Charity had just arrived, but he hadn't taken a sip yet."

I let out the breath I didn't know I was holding. "Thank god."

"Okay, we'd better get out of this place, pronto! Before Maverick's minions see what we've done here." Jareth rises to his feet. He turns to David. "Do you know of an easy way out of here? I hardly think we should walk out the front door."

David shakes his head. "This place is like a maze."

"Don't worry, I'll lead you out."

We all whirl around at the voice in the doorway.

"Frannie!" I cry.

"So did you do it? Did you get the virus?"

"Yes," I said. "And I dusted Maverick, too." Hm, this probably means Francis is out of a job. Hopefully vamps have good unemployment benefits.

David nods over at the pile of ashes formerly known as Maverick. "Thanks to Rayne here, he is no longer a threat to vampkind."

Francis walks over and takes my hand in his. "Thank you, Rayne," he says. "And I'm sure Dana will thank you, too."

"I told you we'd become friends, Frannie," I say with a half-grin, while inside I feel like bursting into tears. It's not fair. All these innocent people and vampires, destroyed because of one vampire's quest for vengeance against an alleged wrong that was committed years and years before.

Francis squeezes me into a big, rib-crushing hug. The guy would have been strong pre-vampire. "You were right," he says, thankfully releasing me. "And now, if you'll just follow me, I'll get you guys out of here."

We follow. He leads us through twisty underground passages and up a set of creaky wooden stairs and through a door. We step out into a warm summer night. The stars are shining. The moon is full. It seems so unfair that in two nights I'll be dead.

"Good luck," Francis says. "I'm going to inform the other vamps what Maverick has done. I'm sure Magnus will have a lot more followers by morning. He turns to me. "And thank you again, Shaniqua."

"My real name's Rayne," I say, reaching up to give him a big hug. "I was using a fake ID to get into the club."

His eyes twinkle. "Really? I never would have known."

"Yeah, yeah."

We say our good-byes and head to Jareth's BMW. David says he's going to go by our house to check on my mother, guard her against any possible repercussions of the slayage and distract her from the fact that her daughter is out way past curfew. I thank him and watch as he walks off into the night. I'm really glad that he turned out to be one of the good guys. Maybe my mom will finally have a chance to be happy.

Jareth and I get into his car; the heated leather seats feel nice against my aching body. He turns the key and then looks at me. "Do you want to go somewhere in particular?" he asks.

"Can we go to the ocean?" I beg, for some reason getting the strangest desire for the sea. Maybe it's because I know I'll never get a chance to see it again. Hear the waves crashing against the shore, smell the salty air, feel the sand crackle between my toes.

He nods and unquestioningly pulls out of his parking space and into the night. We ride silently, as if both lost in our own thoughts, until we get to the beach, about twenty minutes away. We step out of the car and walk down to the end of the boardwalk, toward the ocean. I kick off my shoes and dig my toes into the cool sand. Jareth slips his hand into mine and strokes my fingers.

"So you did it," he says, staring into the blackness of the nighttime sea. There are a thousand stars out and they twinkle like diamonds in the sky. "You accomplished your mission. You're a real slayer now."

"I guess." I shrug. Time to break it to him. "Though a lot of good it's going to do me dead."

Jareth jerks his head around to look at me. "What?" he cries. "What are you talking about?"

I reach up and touch my neck. The bite has scabbed over and even feels diseased and nasty. "Maverick bit me," I say. "And then he injected the virus into my bloodstream. He says I'm going to die in a couple of days. Just like all the donors."

Even in the darkness I can see Jareth's horror-struck face. "Raynie!" he cries and his voice breaks with emotion. He pulls me into a hug, squeezing me with almost as much strength as Francis. But this hug is one of desperation. "Oh, my darling, no!" he murmurs. "I can't lose you."

"Yeah, well, I don't exactly want to be lost either," I say wryly.

Jareth pulls away from the hug, his beautiful blue eyes hardened and angry. "Stop making self-protective jokes," he says. "This is serious. We have to do something."

"What?" I ask. "There's no antidote. Face it. In two to three days, I'll be pushing up daisies." I know I'm being a bitch, but for some reason I'm unable to let go.

Jareth sighs and pulls me down onto the sand. We sit there a moment, not speaking. "You can be so cold and hard," he says at last. "Always putting up a brave front so others don't see your fear. Your vulnerability."

"Maybe I don't want others to see my fear and vulnerability. I mean, it's my fear and vulnerability, right? If I want to keep it inside, then that's my business." I kick at the sand with my foot. "Besides, it's not exactly like you're Mr. Open Up and Share yourself."

"You're right," Jareth says, staring out into the sea. "You and I are a lot alike in many ways. We both have pain in our pasts, which has caused us to put trust in ourselves and not others. But let me tell you, Rayne, from someone who's done it for hundreds of years: It's not a great way to live. And it never gets less lonely." He sighs deeply, lying back into the sand and staring up at the stars. "I never told you why I don't want a blood mate."

I turn to look at him, surprised. This, I was not expecting. Is he ready to spill his deep dark secret at last?

"No," I say slowly. "You never have."

Jareth goes silent. At first I'm almost positive he's not going to speak—that he changed his mind already. But then he opens his mouth.

"Most vampires are turned individually," he says. "But for me, my whole family was vampire."

"Really?" I ask. "That's so cool."

"Yes," he agrees. "You see, my parents and my brother and sister and I were living as peasants in England back during the Black Plague. Terrible time. All our neighbors were dying. The graves were full. You can't imagine the stench of bodies just rotting in the streets, the sulfur from the burnings. We prayed to God that he would rescue us. That he would spare our lives. Well, God sent a dark messenger that day.

"The vamp Runez had come to feed on the sick. Vampires couldn't catch the plague and so it became a good place to feed, without hurting anyone. We didn't have donors back in that day," Jareth explained. "Runez came across my family, huddled in our little hut. Exhausted, hungry, and scared. But not sick. He knew we would soon catch it and suffer terrible deaths. I was eighteen. My little sister was ten and my little brother only four. The vampire felt bad for us and offered us a choice. Immortal life or certain death." Jareth smiled. "Of course, you can guess what we chose."

"So he turned all of you? Isn't that against the rules?" From what I'd read, vamps can only turn one person during their lifetime. Keeps them from having blood shortages like the Red Cross.

"Things were much less organized back then. Vampires roamed the earth, alone and hungry. There were no covens or political parties. We didn't incorporate 'til the early eighteenth century."

"Oh, okay," I say. Interesting. I wonder what (or who) made them all band together. "So then what happened?"

"At first things were great. The five of us escaped the plague and traveled from village to village, taking money from the dead. It sounds terrible, I know. But it was just lying there. Of no use to anyone. Except us. We ended up with enough gold to buy a small castle in southeastern Britain. We bought titles and everyone assumed we were some kind of eccentric royalty. It was then that I trained to be a sculptor. I spent my days carving intricate stone statues to sell to castle courtyards and churches. And since I had eternity to perfect my art, I became quite good. My work can be seen all over Europe, even today.

"In any case, everything had turned out better than our wildest dreams. And best of all, we had each other. A family for eternity. At night we'd gather in the great hall and play games and laugh and laugh." He pauses for a moment, releasing a small sigh. "Sometimes I think I can still hear my sister's giggle, reverberating through a hall."

I smile, thinking of my own family. My silly, hippie-dippy mom, my determined, hard-working sister. If I'd become a vampire I'd totally have wanted to make it a family affair like Jareth did. That way I'd get to keep the people I love around forever.

But Jareth's story, I'm beginning to think, doesn't have such a happy ending.

"Go on," I urge. "What happened next?"

"We lived together for centuries, moving around every few years, as not to arouse the suspicions of the locals. After all, we never grew old. I could, at least, pass for a man, having been turned at eighteen, but my sister and brother were forever children. People began to wonder. And then we'd move." He smiled sadly. "Moving could be tough, but we always had each other. That's all that mattered."

"Right."

"I told you how the vampires came together in the early eighteenth century, right? A great leader, Count Dracul, started the reorganization. He formed covens around the country and assigned each vampire to a specific group. Minigovernments were created in each coven, with the leaders all coming together on one worldwide council. He felt we'd be stronger working together. At first it seemed like a great idea.

"But then, as we grew in strength and wealth, becoming prominent members of society that were numerous enough to control our respective governments, another group rose to stop us." He grimaces. "You might be familiar with them. Slayer Inc."

I grimace back. I'm thinking this is going to be the part where I learn why Jareth is so antislayer.

"Well, Slayer Inc. went to the head vampire consortium and said that while they believed vampires had the right to exist, there should be rules in place so they and humans could peacefully coexist. And they offered to police the ones who did not. I was on the council when the vote came up on whether we wanted to work with them. Since we didn't have a police force of our own and we'd recently seen some really evil vampires causing major havoc, at the time it seemed like a good idea, though not everyone agreed. In the end, the council was split pretty evenly, with me casting the deciding vote."

"In favor of Slayer Inc."

"Yes. It's amazing how one simple vote can change your whole life."

"What happened?"

"Well, after we'd signed the contracts, Slayer Inc. created some rules. Some of these rules were good. We couldn't be running around biting and killing random humans, for example. That's where the donor program was born. Some, however, were . . . not so good."

"What do you mean?"

Jareth swallows hard before speaking. "No children vampires," he says hoarsely. "They said it was an abomination. And that it threatened our secrecy as well, since it's more obvious a child isn't aging."

His voice cracks and he reaches up to swipe a wayward blood tear from his eyes. My heart aches in my chest and I want nothing more than to comfort him, to relieve some of his pain, though I have no idea how. No wonder he holds such a grudge against Slayer Inc. Against me. I'm starting to hate them myself. How could they do that? Kill innocent vampire children? Kill Jareth's brother and sister? What if they had asked me to do the same? Go up to some six-year-old and stake her through the heart? Just like Bertha did with Lucifent. There's no way I could do that. Absolutely no way.

"They came for my brother and sister a week later. We holed ourselves up in our mansion and held out as long as we could. But we ran out of blood and we were dying. Finally, out of desperation, we attempted to fight our way out. It was a massacre. My whole family, besides me, was killed by a rampaging slayer. Because of me and my deciding vote, I lost everyone I ever loved." His voice breaks and he covers his eyes with his hands to hide his tears.

I lie down on my side, placing my head on his solid chest and wrapping my arm around him. He doesn't pull away. "I'm so sorry," I whisper, feeling tears come to my own eyes.

How could anyone move on with their lives after such tragedy? Their whole family slaughtered before their eyes. I try to imagine how that would feel for me—if Sunny and my mother were suddenly cut down for a sin they didn't commit. But I can't. It's just too terrible to comprehend.

Jareth reaches up and strokes the top of my head. His fingers feel light and feathery as they scrape against my scalp. "They believed they were on a crusade against evil," he says sadly. "But my little brother and sister didn't have an evil bone in their bodies." His voice cracks again, and he pauses, swallowing hard before continuing. "They were my everything. My life. My heart. Without them, I had no purpose," he says wearily. "Living forever went from being a gift of the gods to a curse of eternal damnation."

My heart pangs again and I squeeze him closer, a vain attempt to take away even a smidgen of his pain. Poor Jareth. Poor, poor Jareth. No wonder he's so bitter. No wonder he didn't want to give me a chance. I wouldn't have given myself a chance. There's no way I'd have agreed to work side by side with a member of the organization that mercilessly struck down my entire family. *Everyone I had in the world.*

"Of course, soon after the murders, the vampire consortium realized that partnering with Slayer Inc. had been a big mistake," he adds. "Their contracts were taken away and their organization condemned by our kind. But Slayer Inc. grew anyway. And even today, as you know, they feel they have the right to police us." He shakes his head. "So many vampires have died because of me and my vote. If anything, I'm the real vampire slayer."

"But you didn't know," I protest. "You can't blame yourself."

"I gave them the means to exist. The opportunity to slaughter my family and others. How can I not be blamed?"

"Jareth, you have to stop beating yourself up over something that happened so long ago. We all make mistakes. And yes, sometimes the consequences are worse than others, but in the end, you have to forgive yourself and move on."

Jareth sits up, pulling me with him. He cups my face in his hands and meets my eyes with his own earnest ones. "Look, Rayne. I'm sorry I wasn't exactly friendly when we first met. But at least now you know what I'm dealing with. Partnering with a member of Slayer Inc., no matter how sweet she is, just feels so wrong. Like I'm betraying my family in some way. Like once again I'm casting the wrong vote."

I nod. "I understand. I'd hate me, too, I think."

"But then I started to get to know you, against my better judgment. You're not one of them. You have your own set of rights and wrongs, your own code that you live by. I began to fall in love with you. And that scared me to death."

My heart leaps in my chest. In love with me. Jareth is in love with me. He doesn't see me as the pathetic freak who doesn't fit in. The one whose own father doesn't care if she lives or dies. He knows the real me and he loves me. How totally mind-blowing is that?

"I love you, too, Jareth," I whisper. "So much."

He leans forward to kiss me, but I stop him before his lips reach mine. It's torture to do so, but I feel I must.

"Wait. I don't know how contagious I am," I say. "I don't want you to get sick, too."

His face crumbles and I realize for one moment we both forgot my situation. That it doesn't matter who's in love with who because soon there will be no me to be in love with.

"Oh, Rayne," he murmurs, swiping at the bloody tears that spring from the corners of his eyes.

He doesn't need to say anything else. I know exactly what he's thinking. He finally allowed himself to love again, and now he's going to lose again.

Sometimes destiny is, like, so unfair.

# 30

## Vampires Suck

I should have never trusted Jareth. I knew better. I absolutely knew better!

I can't believe I shared all that stuff with him. Opened up for the first time and told him things. Things I haven't told anyone. About my dad. About my failed relationships. About how scared and lonely I am half the time. How I'm sick of pretending I don't care about anything or anyone when I probably care more deeply than anything and anyone I know.

He seemed so genuine. So caring and sweet. He told me his sob story. About his family. Slayer Inc. He told me he was in love with me. He told me he'd stick by my side and not give up. He told me he'd try to find the antidote.

But now he's gone. Disappeared. I'm lying here in my bed, dying, and he's nowhere to be found.

After our night on the beach, the virus kicked in with a vengeance and I've been bedridden ever since, sick as a dog. Everything aches and I'm so weak I can barely sit up. And the only thing I am pining for is Jareth. I want to see him one last time before I die. To feel his hands on me and hear his gentle voice whisper in my ear, telling me everything is going to be okay.

So where the hell is he?

I hate men. Vampires. People in general. You know, in a way I'm effing glad to effing die. At least then the pain will end. The hurt and anguish and suffering that I feel on a daily basis will slip away as I'm carried over the abyss. The soothing waters of death will claim me and everyone will be sorry and they'll cry and say, "Oh what a great girl" when gawking at my body during the wake and funeral. And maybe my dad will show up and he'll be so sorry that he never took the time to know me.

Yeah, my death will serve them right.

# 31

## Waiting for Death

Sorry about that earlier rant. I was just so mad I could hardly see. Or maybe that's just a symptom of the horrible sickness. It's totally taken hold now. I feel like I have mono and the chicken pox and the bubonic plague, all rolled into one. I'm handwriting this, because I'm too weak to sit at the computer.

My mom is freaking-out worried and she doesn't even know the half of it. She takes me to a dozen doctors and they run a ton of tests, but no one can figure out what's wrong with me, of course, and in the end, they just send me home, having no idea this sickness is fatal.

Luckily Mom has David to take care of her. And he's a

master at calming her down. At least I can die knowing I'm not leaving her all alone.

Sunny's a mess, too. Somehow she has figured out a way to blame herself for all of this. If Magnus hadn't bit her by mistake to begin with then I'd be a vampire, not a slayer. And I'd never have been at the Blood Bar, thus Maverick would never have been able to infect me. I try to remind her that then Magnus would have gotten infected through Rachel and Charity and, as his blood mate, I would have gotten infected through him.

In the end, I still die. It seems my destiny. I hope they've got a good backup slayer.

The vamps and Slayer Inc. have been working furiously to come up with an antidote from the virus sample we stole, but haven't had any luck. If they only had more time, they say. But my time is nearly up. If I'm average, I'll probably die tomorrow. If I'm lucky, I may live one more day.

The way I feel right now, I'd rather just die and get it over with.

I've been thinking about death a lot as I lie in my bed, staring up at the ceiling, while everyone hustles around to make sure I have everything I need to be as comfortable as possible. What will it be like? Where will I go? What will people do when I'm gone? Will they follow my wishes and play Bauhaus at my funeral?

My dad hasn't come. That's the most infuriating thing.

I thought for sure when Sunny called him and told him I was dying that he'd be on the next plane. I don't know why. Instead he laughed her off and said she was being overly dramatic.

I hate him.

Him and Jareth.

After Jareth brought me back from the beach, he said he had some things to take care of and that he'd be back. But he hasn't been. And as I lay here dying, the one person my heart aches for is not here. I try not to care. I try to rebuild the wall, as that old band Pink Floyd would have advised. Try to regain my black ice princess shell that Mike Stevens always teases me about. The one where I don't care about anyone or anything. But the ice has melted. I'm vulnerable. Cut open and bleeding.

I listen to the Smiths. The Cure. Depeche Mode. The crooning eighties New Wave singers seem to understand. They're the only ones who do.

Jareth tried to warn me. He said he didn't ever get close to people. He's so similar to me in that respect. Afraid of opening up, of caring for another person. And maybe in a way he's right. He allowed himself to care for his family and they were killed. Now, he allowed himself to care for me and I'm about to kick the bucket myself.

In the end, we all die alone. Maybe it's better to have never loved at all.

Sorry, someone's at the door. More chicken soup, I bet. I'll write more later.

# 32

## Dad. Yes, Dad.

Jareth enters the room and comes to sit in the chair beside my bed. His hair is all tousled, his eyes bloodshot, and it looks like he hasn't slept in days. In fact, if I'm not mistaken he's still wearing the same outfit from the night we went to the Blood Bar.

"Where have you been?" I ask weakly. A few minutes ago I would have rather died than questioned him. Let him know I care. But I'm too sick to be strong, kick-ass Rayne at the moment.

"Vegas," he says.

I raise my eyebrows. "Uh, okay. Win anything?" I can't believe he was off gambling as I lay dying. I mean, I know poker is hot and all, but couldn't he have waited a couple days for that straight flush?

"I got what I went for, if that's what you mean."

"What, a lap dance?"

He chuckles. "Even sick, you're still funny, Rayne."

"Barrel of laughs, that's me," I say sarcastically, closing my eyes. I've become real sensitive to light these days and even more sensitive to seeing Jareth.

"Open your eyes, Rayne," Jareth commands.

Reluctantly I obey. Then open them even wider when I see what—I mean who—is standing behind Jareth.

"Dad?" I croak hoarsely. Am I hallucinating now?

"Hi, kiddo. I'm so sorry you're not feeling well."

For a moment, I'm still not convinced he's real as he walks over to my bed and sits down on the side. He's older looking then I remember, a little gray at his temples and in his beard. But overall, he still looks the same. Still looks like my dad.

I turn to look back at Jareth. "How . . . ?" I ask.

Dad smiles down at me. "This man of yours is very convincing, Rayne. He showed up at my doorstep one evening and said I had to come with him. That you needed me."

My heart pangs in my chest. Here I was blaming Jareth for disappearing and all along he'd been out hunting for the one thing he knew I needed more than anything.

"I'll leave you two to talk," the vampire says, walking to the door.

"Jareth," I call after him. He stops and turns back to look at me. "Thank you," I say.

He smiles the sweetest smile and nods, before turning and walking out the door. I smile back, my heart overflowing. God, I love that vampire. At least when I die, I'll die in love.

I turn back to my dad, noticing a few beads of sweat have formed on his forehead even though it's definitely not too hot in my room. He's nervous. Well, he damn well should be, after what he's done. And just because he's here now, doesn't mean I will let him off the hook.

"Thanks for coming," I say, forcing myself to be civil.

"Rayne, I'm so sorry to hear you've been sick. What do the doctors say? Is there anything they can do? A hospital we can send you to? Anything. I'll pay whatever it costs. Just tell your mother to send me the bill. I want you to get better."

He sounds so concerned. Is this what it had to take? I had to die to get his attention?

"The doctors don't know what's wrong," I say wearily. It really is an effort to talk today. "There's nothing they can do."

"Oh, my darling," he says, his voice breaking. "I hate to see you like this."

"You hate to see me at all, apparently."

"What's that supposed to mean?"

"Uh, hello? Birthday party? Balloons and presents and cake? Last week? Any of that ring a bell to you?"

His face crumbles. "I'm a terrible father," he says, staring down at his hands. I realize he's developed liver spots. He can't be old enough to have liver spots, can he?

"I'm not saying that," I protest, though, of course, I have been saying that all week. But it's unbearable for me to see him look so guilty. "It's just . . . well, we haven't seen you in years, Dad. And we were . . . looking forward to it."

A war is raging inside of me at this point. The old Rayne wants to be bitter and hateful and sarcastic and mean. She wants to cut him down and make him feel the hurt that she's felt because of him. To make him think she doesn't give a crap that he didn't show because he means absolutely nothing to her.

But the new Rayne, the one that is loved by Jareth, wonders if she has the strength to be honest with him. To admit that he hurt her and give him the chance to make things right. The new Rayne wonders if he has a reason for his actions. The new Rayne wonders if he, too, walks around with a hard shell of indifference to hide his inner turmoil.

The new Rayne knows that this man gave life to her. And that he may not have always been there, but he's there now. The new Rayne wants to give him a chance.

"You hurt my feelings when you didn't show," I admit, dying inside at the admission. Before today I wouldn't have told anyone that ever. But in a weird way, as soon as I say it, I feel a little better. "I waited for you until one A.M. The others all went to bed. I was sure you'd walk through that door with a birthday cake in hand. I believed in you, Dad. And you let me down."

Dad nods slowly, still staring at his hands. His eyes blink a few times too fast and I wonder if he's holding back tears. Tears! I never, ever thought in a million years I'd see my dad cry.

"Rayne, I can't do anything but apologize to you for that," he says at last, his voice sounding more than a bit froggy. "I feel so terrible. It's just . . . well, I got scared."

I raise an eyebrow. "Scared?"

"I know I've been a lousy dad. Running away from responsibility and family and everyone who loved me. Your mother, who has always been so sweet. You and Sunny, the most wonderful daughters a father could ever hope for. I felt, somehow, that I didn't deserve you. I'm so rotten inside, Rayne. I've done terrible things. And I felt that by leaving I would protect you two from all of that. I knew your mother would take care of you. Raise you right. You didn't need me screwing everything up." He shrugs. "Basically I got scared. Weird, huh? Scared because suddenly people needed me. Because they loved me. Sounds so dumb when I say it out loud."

It's at that moment I realize how much he really is my dad. And it makes me burst into tears. "Dad, I don't need you. But I do love you," I admit. "I've always loved you. That's why it hurts so much when you stay away."

"I've been feeling guilty about the whole thing for so

long," Dad continues. "Then your sister sent me that e-mail about your birthday and I realized that was my chance to make things right. I mean, coming to a birthday doesn't make up for four years of wrongs, but I thought perhaps it'd be a start. A chance to reconnect with you two and come back into your lives." He swallows hard. "But then I got the e-mail back from Sunny when I accepted her invitation. She sounded so happy, so excited. I panicked again. I didn't know what I was doing. How I'd be able to face you two after all that had happened. So I took the coward's way out. I didn't show."

He scrubs his face with his hands. "I'm so sorry, Raynie girl. I screwed everything up, once again. And now here I am and you're so sick and I don't want to lose you."

It takes all my strength to sit up in bed, but I do it. Because right at this moment I need a hug. A hug from my father. I put out my arms and he wraps his around me, pulling me close. He squeezes me into the big bear hug I remember as a kid, though today his arms don't seem as strong. Probably because he's shaking. I bury my head in his shoulder and cry.

"I love you, Daddy," I sob. "I don't care what you've done or what you will do in the future. I'll always love you."

"Thank you, Raynie," he says. "I love you, too. No matter what, you'll always be my baby girl."

"Dad?" I ask, as I pull away and lie back down on the bed. Sitting up takes way too much energy. "Will you do me a favor?"

"Anything."

"Tell me a story. Like you used to."

He smiles, his eyes crinkling, and I can definitely see the tears now. "Of course," he says, his voice quavering a bit. "Once upon a time, there lived two princesses—Sunshine and Rayne. . . ."

# 33

## The Sacrifice

After Dad leaves I take a nap, feeling both emotionally and physically drained. But for the first time since I came down with the disease I sleep peacefully. No haunting nightmares. And I wake up feeling better. Yes, I will die, but I will die with much more peace than I had for most of my life.

A knock on the door. I say, "Come in."

It's Jareth.

"How was your dad?" he asks, sitting on the side of my bed. He presses a cold hand against my burning forehead. I close my eyes.

"Wonderful. I'll never be able to thank you enough for tracking him down."

"It was nothing. I'd do anything for you," he says sincerely.

I open my eyes. "Have you heard from the lab?"

He hangs his head. "Yes. Unfortunately they have not been able to come up with an antidote. At least not yet. If only they had more time."

I sigh, resigning myself once more to my impending death. For some reason I had been keeping a small hope alive deep inside that they'd be able to save me in the nick of time, like it always happens in the movies. But I guess, in this case, it was not meant to be.

"Listen, Rayne, there is one possibility," Jareth says hesitantly.

"Huh?" I look up at him.

"I took a lock of your hair and had them test it. You and I are compatible."

"Compatible?"

"As blood mates. We have compatible DNA."

I stare at him, confused. "But what do you—?"

He swallows hard. "I could turn you. Then you would live. Well, not live exactly. Your body would die. But you would be immortal."

"But if you bite me, you'll get the disease. You'll become weak and lose all your vampire powers. Won't you?"

"Yes."

"But then . . . how . . . ?"

Jareth takes my hand in his and pulls it up to his lips. He

kisses it softly, his mouth caressing my sensitive skin. "I love you, Rayne," he murmurs. "You're the first person I've met since my family was killed that I have opened up to. The first person I've allowed myself to care for. You and I are a lot alike in that respect. We live shallow, empty, solo lives because we live in fear of getting too close to another. But together, I think we can do better than that."

He lowers my hand and looks into my eyes. "I want to be with you for eternity. I want to share everything with you."

I can't believe it. I can scarcely believe it. Jareth wants me! Little old screwed up and scarred me. And he wants to turn me into a vampire. My dream come true.

"But you didn't answer my question. What about the virus? Won't you catch it?"

He nods. "Yes. It's most likely that I will. But don't you see?" he cries. "I don't care. I'd rather be weak and powerless and with you than lose you. None of this world means a thing to me if you're not there to share it."

"Really?" Hot tears burn my cheeks and for once I let them fall, unchecked. "You really mean that?"

"With all my heart." He reaches over to stroke my sweaty forehead. "Please, Raynie, don't leave me. Say you will be mine forever."

"But I don't want you to lose your powers. . . ."

He shakes his head, smiling down at me. "Will you stop arguing with me for once in your life and just do what I say?"

I grin. "*May*be."

"Then say you'll be mine. Say you'll let me take you as my blood mate. Say that you'll stay with me for eternity."

"If you're sure you want me."

"I'm very sure."

"Then okay." I laugh and realize suddenly I'm also crying. "What the heck, right?"

He leans down and finds my neck, his breath against my skin. I remember the first time he bit me in the Blood Bar. How good it felt. But the sensation is nothing compared to this intimate moment. What was once just physically appealing is now something more. There's love in his bite and as he releases the vampire blood into my veins his mind opens to me and I can feel all that he feels. Know all that he knows.

I can feel his pain. His hurt and loneliness. I understand his bitterness and his sorrow. But there's something else there now. A radiant hope and joy that's more powerful than the hurt. A flash of soft, glowing light that envelops my body and steals away all my pain.

I pass out and when I wake up I'm feeling good enough to sit up in bed. I see Jareth still sitting by my bedside and I wonder how long I've been unconscious. He smiles at me.

"How are you feeling?" he asks.

"A lot better, actually," I say, surprised. I sit up in bed and don't feel dizzy.

"Good. It may take a few days for my blood to fully bond with your own."

"Yeah. I remember Sunny had a week before the transformation would have been completed."

"Of course, you won't gain any of the vampire powers. We're basically gimped pseudovamps now."

My thoughts sober at this. "I'm sorry you had to do that," I say. "I mean, I hate that I'm responsible for—"

"Are you kidding?" Jareth asks. "This is the best day of my life." He cups my face in his hands and kisses me softly on the mouth. "I love you, Rayne," he says. "And now I can have you for eternity."

"I love you, too, Jareth."

We kiss for a moment, then he pulls away. "Oh!" he cries. "I almost forgot!" He reaches down under the bed and pulls out a box. He lifts the lid.

Chocolate cake. Just like the one Dad was supposed to bring.

"Happy vampire birthday, my dear," he says.

Did I mention how much I love this guy?

# Epilogue

So that's my story. A few days later I'm good as new and out of bed. My mom is surprised by my miraculous recovery, but David is able to convince her not to look a gift horse in the mouth and bring in the doctors again. Which is good, considering I think they'd probably be pretty freaked out if they started testing me. Of course, in a few years, when I don't look any older than seventeen still, she and I are going to have to sit down and have a little chat.

That should be fun. *Not.*

Sunny and Magnus are overjoyed at my recovery and Mag doesn't even seem that pissed that he's lost his best vampire general. He's got others in line, he says, and is much more interested in Jareth's and my happiness than in some military position. Oh, and bonus—I've convinced Magnus to re-examine the coven's policy for letting outside vamps into the ranks. Frannie and Dana are definitely in. And many of their friends may soon get their membership cards in the mail as well.

My dad stays until I'm fully better and when he leaves, he tells me I'm welcome to visit him anytime and that he wants to be a part of our lives again. And this time I know he means it.

Oh, and one of the unexpected side benefits? I may not have vampire powers, but I also don't have a lot of their downsides. For some reason the virus seems to have bonded with the melatonin in the skin and Jareth and I are able to face the sunlight without fear of burning to a crisp. This is an even bigger deal to Jareth, seeing as he hasn't caught a glimpse of the sun in nearly a thousand years.

And as for Jareth and me, well, we're just great. To think I actually had to lose my soul to find my soulmate. But hey, whatever works, right? And who really gives a care about vampire powers when we have each other? We have a blast just being together. And we make a point to share everything—even when it's difficult. No secrets between us, that's the only way this is going to work out.

Summer passes without event and soon it's time for school to start again. Sadly, since I'm not allergic to the sun, I'm also not exempt from attending high school. But I guess that's okay. After all, I've got eternity. Might as well get myself educated.

So one September day I'm walking through Oakridge High, dressed in my goth best, making fun of the cheerleaders, ducking away from the teachers who I owe assignments to, etc., etc. Your typical Raynie day. When all of a sudden I hear a *Psst* sound from the side corridor. I turn to look and see Mr. Teifert waving madly at me from down the hall.

"You must come with me," he says in an urgent voice.

I've technically retired from the slayer biz, by the way. The virus made me too weak to perform my duties. But Teifert says once a slayer, always a slayer and you never know when they might need me. And from the look on his face, I'm thinking this may be one of those times.

Great. And here I thought all I'd have to worry about this semester was Calculus.

"What's up, T?" I ask, as I approach him.

"Rayne, we have a problem, and we need your help."

"Of course you do." I sigh. "What is it this time?"

"It's Mike Stevens."

"Mike Stevens?" I scowl at the name of my captain-of-the-football-team nemesis. I'd almost managed to forget about him over the summer. "What about Mike Stevens?"

"He's missing."

"Uh, okay, T," I say. "Let's get something straight here. Mike Stevens missing doesn't necessarily qualify as a problem.

I mean, have you met the guy? Some might say a missing Mike Stevens could be the best thing to happen to Oakridge in a long time."

"That's not all," Teifert says. "There's also something suddenly very odd about the cheerleaders."

"Odd about the cheerleaders?" I cock my head. "You mean more odd than usual about a group of girls who wants to dance and kick up their legs while wearing short skirts in the middle of a New England November?"

"Yes. And, Rayne, this is going to sound weird, but . . ."

"Dude, after all I've been through, nothing's going to sound weird. Absolutely nothing in the known universe."

"The cheerleaders? They've been heard, uh . . . growling."

Huh. Then again . . . maybe I'm wrong.

*To be continued . . .*